PRAISE FOR ALLA CRONE'S BOOKS

East Lies the Sun

Gold Medal winner of *West Coast Review of Books*

"... was an immediate success ... an exciting book ... historically accurate."

Santa Rosa Press Democrat

"Alla Crone's byline will be eagerly sought by readers ... the book brims with the authentic flavor of the time..."

Sonoma Index Tribune

Rodina

"Alla Crone has a gift for creating a sense of place, whether it is Shanghai during the bombing of 1937, or San Francisco in 1947 ... The author also creates the ominous atmosphere of the Cold War. The historical crisis intensifies her (the heroine's) own dilemma as a woman without a country. There are stormy passions here... Vickie is a survivor ..."

The Press Democrat

Winds Over Manchuria

"... is written with the style and tradition of Ayn Rand"

Book Reviews, L'Affaire de Coeur

Legacy of Amber

"Alla Crone successfully blended the political, cultural and romantic themes making her story work on all levels."

Publishers Weekly

North of the Moon

"Three novels about history, culture and romance in the Soviet Union have propelled Alla Crone into national attention ... *North of the Moon* captures the sweep and passion of the period and the authenticity is remarkable ..."

San Mateo Times

The Other Side of Life

"Alla Crone has attempted to take us into the unknown ...What happens when we die? Do all our hopes and dreams end in a second? Are the lessons learned in one lifetime? These questions and the personal connections of her characters make this a fascinating read."

Linda Loveland Reid, author of *Touch of Magenta*

"It's a gripping novel, riveting in so many ways. Alla Crone describes so deftly the setting, whether in the out-of-doors — breathtaking, the finest writing — or in one of her lavish court scenes. If you resonate with the poetry of her prose you will delight in this novel. If you relish being transported to the palaces of princes and kings, this novel will send you thither. It is heart-warming, mind-bending, soul-engaging trip."

Patsy Garlan, author, Viking Press, Prentice Hall
The Atlantic Monthly

Captive of Silence

"Alla Crone's *Captive of Silence* is written with an eloquence that is hard to find in writing. She captures the time period with finesse. To tell such a difficult story in such a compelling way is an art that Crone has mastered. Towards the end, I could not put this book down. Crone's writing is honest, poignant and genuine. I highly recommend her book, especially to learn history in a fascinating way and to be inspired by a person who can rise above and learn from an abusive and extremely difficult life."

Marlene Cullen, *The Write Spot Books*

"Alla Crone has written a touching, poignant novel... that reads like an autobiography. Told in the first person by Nina who speaks to us as her confidants about her life from birth to the present, we learn her most intimate secrets... Her family was an eyewitness to the Russian Revolution, to the Russian outpost in Manchuria, to Shanghai during the Japanese occupation in WW II. A powerful and courageous novel."

Kate Farrell, author

Russian Bride

"It is so refreshing to read a work that is completely true to the characters. Although the heroine of this book suffers a lot and often feels uncomfortable or confused, her actual self is always on the page, making the reader identify with the heroine, feel for her and yet admire her. This book covers a long life, is located in several different countries and contains characters one doesn't usually meet — a Russian mother, an army colonel, an immigrant who has the world of America before her but must adjust to all the vagaries of another culture. The book is beautifully and honestly written and touches the heart as well as the mind. I urge readers to immerse themselves in the life of a Russian bride for all it can tell them about relationships, assimilation and the pains and rewards of adjustment to a new life."

Ellen Boneparth, author of *Unwanted*

"*Russian Bride* is a fiction based on fact novel. Nina was born into a wealthy family in the Russian community in Harbin, Manchuria. When her parents lost everything Nina experienced deprivation, humiliation and discovered an inner strength that led her to a new world with Colonel Richard Allan, a physician in the U.S. Army Air Corps. This is a love story that leads the handsome couple from China to a fascinating lifestyle in the United States. This is a story rich in detail about what it's like to traverse this rocky terrain of a unique community to strange new world. It's also a story of the fragility and complex nature of human beings. Nina maneuvers the tricky challenges of pleasing her demanding mother and haughty mother-in-law.

"I thoroughly enjoyed the adventure into a world foreign to me. Alla Crone eloquently writes in a style that is engaging and transports the reader to a myriad of situations, places and important historical events. An engaging travelogue, attentive of the complexities of relationships and details of the era result in a satisfying story. All in a day's work for our courageous heroine."

Marlene Cullen, *The Write Spot Books*

Also by Alla Crone

Secret Station
Russian Bride
Captive of Silence
The Other Side of Life
Maxim
Rodina
Legacy of Amber
North of the Moon
Winds over Manchuria
East Lies the Sun

Acknowledgement

Thank you, Karen Ely, for your meticulous and enthusiastic work on this book.

NEMESIS

A Novel

Alla Crone

Nemesis
A Novel

© 2020 Alla Crone

ISBN: 978-1-941066-46-1

Book design by Jo-Anne Rosen

Wordrunner Press
Petaluma, California

To Marlene Cullen

My remarkable editor and friend,

who kept me on the right path.

"Truth is not only violated by falsehood; it may be equally outraged by silence. "

—*Amiel*

AUTHOR'S NOTE

The description of an American Consulate, its environment, and its staff in Harbin Manchuria between the years 1909 and 1939 is fiction. Any resemblance to persons living or dead is purely coincidental.

NEMESIS

Chapter 1

Harbin, Manchuria
October 26, 1909

*Residents of Harbin marveled at the mild end of October. The eve-
ning was clear, and the face of the full moon seemed to share its smile
with pedestrians and guards standing in a semicircle on the platform
near the area they estimated first class would stop. No fanfare was
planned for the arrival of the Japanese Admiral Ito Hiroshumi who
was expected to come for a meeting with Vladimir Kokovtsov, a
representative of Imperial Russia in Manchuria.*

*One of the guards yawned broadly as the train crawled by and
stopped exactly where the guards thought it would. The admiral
stepped down to the platform and returned the waiting men's salute.
No one noticed a man in dark clothes walk up until he stopped in
front of the admiral and shot him three times, then turned on the
guards and shot all three before vanishing into the darkness behind
the station. By the time the ambulance and the police arrived, the
admiral and the guards were dead.*

∽

Outside the main entrance of Harbin railway station, one
of the few paved roads led to the top of a hill dominated by a
Russian Orthodox Cathedral. Built entirely of wood, it was a

favorite place of worship for Russian residents, especially those living within walking distance of the church. Several streets fanned out from there, hiding homes among a variety of trees and shrubbery. The white and gray stone houses in other parts of uptown shared the streets with the elaborately designed mansions of the affluent government officials. The downtown business buildings, department stores, and hotels used various architectural designs, and had their signs in Russian. Street names throughout the city were also in Russian, making Harbin look almost like a European city located in Manchuria, were it not for the presence of trotting rickshaw coolies and Chinese beggars sitting on sidewalks whining for alms.

Two mansions, of similar architecture, stood close to each other on a side street near the Cathedral. The one with ionic pillars on the portico belonged to a 32-year-old-bachelor, Anton Platonov, who was the owner of a large brewery which he inherited from his parents, who had died seven years earlier from influenza. The industrious heir was now rich enough to own half of Harbin.

The other mansion with Doric pillars belonged to his 47-year-old-neighbor and friend, Vassili Melnikov, less affluent, yet wealthy enough as a high-ranking executive at the local bank. Although a doting father to his 20-year old daughter, Lisa, he was also fond of playing poker. His grief over his wife, who died in childbirth, guided him to the gambling tables, to which he had become addicted, and where he spent long hours away from home. His other recreation was big game hunting, and for this he used to go to Korea where he successfully hunted boar.

Much as he loved his daughter, Vassili left her most of the day in the care of his servants, with the result that at her young age, Lisa was more mature than her classmates, well familiar with how to care for the house and cooking her father's favorite dishes. There came a time, however, when her father told her she needed a governess to teach her French and English as well as a lady's proper manners. Lisa adamantly refused and demanded a private teacher instead. Vassili resisted for a while and finally succumbed to his daughter's plea. He hired Mrs. Glebova, a middle-aged, retired schoolteacher and a genteel widow with graying hair, who lived a short distance from them in a small house. She came every weekday in the afternoons when Lisa was home from school. After teaching French or English grammar on alternate days, Mrs. Glebova took Lisa out for a walk, speaking with her either in French or English on any given day. It wasn't long before the young girl picked up the rudiments of each language and enjoyed her daily walks.

Early on, Mrs. Glebova introduced Lisa to poetry and made her memorize various stanzas. While her classmates struggled with it, Lisa loved the music of poetic rhythm and the lulling sound of rhyming lines. Then came the French La Fontaine, followed by English Lord Tennyson. She loved them all, but the Russian poetry sang to her, especially Pushkin and Lermontov. When her girlfriends used their leisure time chatting over intricate needlepoint, Lisa always found reasons to be busy somewhere else. She loved analyzing and comparing various poets in the way they composed their rhyming stanzas, and often lost herself in her favorite pastime.

On the day of the Admiral Ito Hiroshumi's arrival, Lisa took part in setting a festive table for an elaborate dinner her father was planning for the Admiral the next day. Vassili had become his friend during one of his hunting trips to Korea, when several boars stampeded out of the woods into the city, scattering scared pedestrians into side streets. Careless about his own safety, Vassili started chasing the boars, and was getting close enough to shoot, when the police overtook him, handcuffed, and put him in prison instead, without being accused of anything. Had it not been for the admiral's astute judgement of Vassili's innocence, he could have been languishing in prison much longer.

And now, two years later, the admiral was due to arrive in Harbin to be feted in Vassili's mansion.

Chapter 2

Lisa was a tall, graceful beauty with large brown eyes and luxurious, chestnut hair. By the time she reached her twentieth year, Mrs. Glebova had become a good family friend, and accompanied her as a chaperone to many receptions at the American Consulate. It was there that Lisa met David Jones, a twenty-four-year-old attaché, at one of their receptions. His erect figure, blond hair brushed smoothly off his face, and a pair of twinkling blue eyes beckoned her to him irresistibly. He courted her with intensity, flattering the unsophisticated and naïve Lisa, who responded by falling in love with the young man.

She was always chaperoned by Mrs. Glebova who, after leaving Lisa to dance inside the consulate, joined her American counterpart, who enjoyed watching the young people having a good time. Lisa taught David to dance the polka, and mazurka, and David in turn, showed her the intricate and sexy movements of the popular tango, which took her breath away when he moved to dance cheek to cheek. Her body fused with his, and she followed his movements in rhythm with the music.

At one of the dinner dances, tipsy with love, Lisa tried to decline yet another drink, but when she saw that it was Veuve Clicquot Demi-Sec, her father's favorite, she couldn't resist it, and enjoyed too much of its smooth, slightly sweet taste. One glass followed another, and before long she succumbed to David's coaxing to visit his apartment.

"Come on, Lisa, don't be such a perennial little coward," David teased her with his seductive smile she knew so well. "You have to see what I was able to rent with my consulate allowance for housing." "I'm not a coward... but I don't think... she would approve," Lisa said, forming the words with difficulty and nodding toward the chaperone. "Oh, look, she's absorbed in listening to her counterpart, she won't notice. Come on!"

Somewhere inside her befuddled brain, a nagging thought needled her that what David was suggesting should be avoided, but the curiosity to see his place won over, and she followed him, sneaking away from Mrs. Glebova who was, as David had pointed out, deep in conversation with an American chaperone.

～

The next morning, she couldn't remember what happened after a tour of David's apartment or how she got home. Only brief snippets of what went on inside David's bedroom surfaced. They were kisses, caresses, and a blissfully fading conscience on a wave of submission.

Lisa promptly sat up in her bed. How far did she allow him to go? There was only one way to find out. She threw off her duvet and ran to her bathroom, where she wiped herself with a moist towel. The evidence and sensitivity were irrefutable, and Lisa collapsed back on her bed, horrified. *Oh, God, what have I done?* Panting and struggling to unravel her thoughts, one more mortifying than the other, Lisa came out of the bathroom and slumped on her bed. The worst thing was that she couldn't do anything but wait, harboring her secret alone, until next time she would see David.

But the next day she couldn't wait any longer and went to the consulate. David took her to an empty office and asked her what brought her back to the consulate. "The night in your apartment, did you . . . did you know I was . . . innocent?" Lisa couldn't look at his handsome face. "Not until it was too late. But we're in love and no one has to know what goes on in my apartment. We're not the only ones who have affairs here. We can continue to meet in my place until we are ready to tell your father of our love." David tried to lift her chin up, but she resisted. "This coming Saturday there's going to be a small cocktail party and you must come as my guest. We'll talk then, but now I've slipped out of a conference and must get back." David kissed her on her forehead and left the room.

Lisa knew that her father's dream was to find a well-situated young man in some industry not far from where they lived and have his daughter near him. So, she kept her relationship with David secret. Reassured by his undisturbed reaction, she accepted all invitations to the consulate, enjoying her affair with David, and living for the moment.

⤳

A while earlier, Lisa had learned of their neighbor Anton Platonov's project to protect the trees inside his property, both deciduous and evergreens, by nurturing them and saving them from being cut down. Loving the trees herself, she joined his work, unaware of Anton's deep affection for her. The evening before the dinner for the Admiral, sitting next to Anton in his garden, she raised her head and watched the slivered moon peeking through the leaves that seemed to shake in a playful resistance to an aggressive breeze.

Lisa laughed. "The birch leaves chasing the wind away!" Anton smiled with an indulging look at her. "You have a vivid imagination, my dear. You should try writing a poem about it. Trees and leaves have lives of their own as you well know."

"Well, it's a bit scary to think of being watched by them when we don't know it. Birch is my favorite, but blue spruce is so majestic that I always look at it in awe. I think it's a crime to cut it down for Christmas, when there are plenty of other trees available. You have such a lush garden compared to ours. Papa doesn't care for gardening, so we leave it in its natural condition, just trying to keep it tidy." Lisa looked down at her watch. "Oh, my goodness, I have overstayed my welcome! I have to get home to help Papa. We're having a reception for the Admiral tomorrow. Papa knows him from his hunting days in Korea, where the Admiral was serving as Resident General. No official reception is planned, but Papa likes him and wants to honor him privately." Lisa bid Anton good-night, and rushed home.

The next morning, she was awakened by loud knocking on her door and her father's frantic voice, "Lisa, Lisa! Get up! The admiral was killed last night!"

"Oh, my God!" cried Lisa, throwing off her duvet and putting on her robe and slippers. "I'm coming, Papa!" she called, opening the door and hugging her father.

"I've ordered the servants to remove all preparations for today's reception ... *Boje moi!* My God! What are we going to do?"

"What's the matter Papa, why are you so upset?"

Her father winced and rubbed his forehead. "You won't understand, *dyetka,* it's too complicated."

Lisa always hated her father calling her by this diminutive name of 'child,' but she ignored it this time and persisted, "Try me! I'm grown up now."

Vassili wiped his face with a handkerchief and looked at his daughter as if seeing her for the first time. "Well, the admiral had resigned from his post in Korea as Resident General because the

Japanese government planned to annex Korea while he wanted it to be absorbed by Japan. He came to consult with the Russian representative here, but he was still looked upon by our population with suspicion, after we lost the Russo-Japanese-war in 1905. But I always found him a stellar character and we became friends. I never told you this, and now I have to be careful with the local authorities."

"Well, Papa, the servants will remove everything from the dining room in time and they will be silent. We never called the admiral by name."

After Lisa got dressed and came down, her father led her to the parlor. "Sit down, I have something else to tell you, of which I'm ashamed. You know that I like to gamble for recreation."

Lisa nodded, tightening her fists on her knees, waiting for the next sentence.

"I let my good sense go trying to win back what I had lost at gambling, but instead I kept losing all that I had." Vassili put his hand on the mantle to steady himself. "Determined to turn my luck, I took money from the bank, sure to win this time--"

Lisa interrupted, "And?"

"I lost it all, and the worst of it is that I can't return the money, so I am an embezzler." Head in his hands, Vasilli sat down in the armchair. Lisa noticed that her father's face was ashen as he spoke, so she said, "Well, is there anything you can do to solve the problem?"

Vassili shook his head. "Not yet. As things stand now, as soon as the bank discovers my crime, I'll go to prison, unless ..."

"Yes?" prompted Lisa, holding her breath, because this reluctance of her father to speak was so uncharacteristic of him that she was now scared.

Vassili shook his head. "Unless I do something I hate doing."

"And what is that, Papa?"

"Ask our friend, Anton, for a loan which, he will know I won't be able to return for a long time, if ever."

"Ask him, Papa, he is your best friend, he won't refuse you, I am sure."

Vassili lowered his head. "Oh, God, I'm so ashamed…" With that, he shook his head and left the room.

Lisa waited for her father's return for a good two hours, imagining all kinds of reasons for such a long visit at Anton's. She had breakfast of a cup of coffee with her favorite sesame bread and returned to her bedroom until finally Vassili showed up. He was ashen and staggered toward a reclining chair which Lisa used to read in before going to sleep. He unbuttoned his shirt collar, wiped his forehead with a handkerchief and looked at his daughter with reddened eyes.

"Come, pull up a chair, *dyetka*, and listen to me without interrupting, please."

Again, Lisa did not correct her father about calling her with her childish diminutive name, sensing that something far more important was on her father's mind.

"Lisa, my precious child, hear me out to the end before you react. I beg you …" Lisa reached over and put her hand on his arm. "Papa, please … I'm ready to listen … what is it that you have to tell me?"

Vassili took Lisa's hands in his. "You know how much I admire Anton and treasure his friendship, so when I told him I needed to borrow money from him, he raised his hand to stop me and said he did not need to know the details. He then went to get a check from his desk, asking how much I needed. When I told him, he put down the pen and slowly turned around in his armchair to face me. He then said he had to talk to his financial advisor as to which of his investments would be best to sell."

"He was gone for a while, and when he came back, I was relieved to see him smiling. His advisor told him cashing some of his investments would damage his portfolio and he should look for a tangible collateral." Vassili coughed, cleared his throat, and looked away.

"What about ..." Lisa started, but Vassili held up his hand. "I'm not finished. There's more." He took her hand in his. "I almost cannot say this. Anton laughed and said, 'Don't worry, the collateral I'm asking for is Lisa's hand in marriage, provided she agrees of course, and then all your problems will be solved.'"

Lisa's mouth dropped open. "Marry Anton? He is twelve years older than I! What did you tell him?"

"I brought up the age difference, but he wouldn't change. But he said 'provided she agrees.'"

"I know he's not a bad person because I do want you to marry him. Think about it, *dyetka*. Such a large sum ... even though Anton is a generous man, I will always feel ashamed. Please, my wise daughter. Do what I beg you to do. Agree to marry Anton. Take time to see what is at stake here if you refuse, and I can't find another collateral ... it's arrest and prison for me!"

Lisa excused herself and hurried out of the room. Her stomach churned and she barely made it to the bathroom where she emptied her stomach. After cleaning her face, she looked at herself in the mirror. Dark circles under her eyes attested that she hadn't been sleeping well. There was no escaping her suspicion that she was pregnant with David's child. She had been nauseated for several mornings and simply refused to admit it.

She leaned on the sink with both hands and tried to assess her options, but no matter how much she tried to avoid the obvious, she knew she was trapped. Lisa had developed a practical streak in her character, helping her father manage the household help and controlling the budget, even though she was so young.

Now she walked away from the sink and sat down on the padded stool near the bathtub. She had to marry Anton and she had to hide her pregnancy, especially from David. She knew she had to accept Anton's proposal and plan the wedding as soon as possible.

There was no use arguing with her father. She couldn't consider letting him go to prison. Until now she was quite fond of Anton as a dear friend, but now she had to convince him that she was not forced to accept him but was quite willing to become his wife. She closed her eyes and brought Anton's image in her mind's eye. For the first time she realized that he was actually quite handsome, with no trace of gray in his dark hair, and had a twinkle in his brown eyes. After all, he was thirty-two years old and it would be some years yet before age would manifest itself. She had never seen him without a tie and a well-coordinated vest under a tweed jacket. In fact, Lisa used Anton as an example of a perfectly groomed gentleman whenever her father's disheveled sandy hair and daily wrinkled clothes annoyed her, ever since nanny Masha told her that he seemed to lose his previous joie de vivre when his wife died. Lisa knew she should not condemn him for his weakness at the card tables. There were worse vices to which her father could have fallen victim.

As soon as he would leave for the bank, she had to call their family physician. Dr. Semenov had been a good friend and would understand her problem. It would be a definite conclusion and she would have to deal with her future from then on. She couldn't delay. Tomorrow she would ask Anton if she could visit him.

Chapter 3

There was also David to deal with. How could she convince him of her change of heart, two weeks after their last rendezvous full of passion? No. She had to stay as close to the truth as she could. She would tell him about her father's bad investments and future revenues, and then reveal the unexpected proposal from Anton.

But first, she had to see Anton from a different point view. Except for their age difference, she had much more in common with him than with David. In fact, the only similarity was their age — David was 24 and she was 20. Was passion enough to substitute for everything else? Of course not. How could she have allowed herself to be swept off her feet by the young American? Easy. The glamor of a foreign country was tantalizing in their proximity to David.

Alone in her room, she began to laugh. My God, she thought, I had been planning to marry David, whose color of eyes I can't remember! Her laughter was becoming louder and louder, until it turned into hysterical gasps and subsided into quiet weeping.

"Barinya! Barinya!"

The maid's anxious voice made Lisa sit up. Loyal Masha, she thought, wiping her face in a hurry. "Come in, Masha!"

When the maid's anxious face showed in the opened door, Lisa forced a smile. "Help me dress, I am in a hurry on an important errand."

Masha started to pick up Lisa's clothes, scattered all over the room, and stealing furtive glances at Lisa's face.

"Don't fret, Barinya," she said to her mistress, "I think Barin was worried about this admiral business." Masha draped a dinner dress over her arm and looked at Lisa. "A few minutes ago, two policemen came and asked him to follow them. They didn't arrest him, were polite, but took him anyway. We are all loyal here and nobody is going to talk. We know how to keep our tongues behind our teeth."

Lisa chose a day dress from her wardrobe, ignoring Masha's love of using Russian sayings at every opportunity, thus embellishing her simple vocabulary. She was glad Masha was there helping her dress, but now there was the worry about her father being taken by the Chinese police. How long would they keep questioning him before he convinced them this would have been just a social visit by the admiral?

But first of all, she had to see Dr. Semenov and get the right answer about her pregnancy.

She hoped the doctor's waiting room would be empty, but no such luck. Three other patients were already waiting to be seen ahead of her, two women and one man. Lisa picked up the newspaper, but her hands were trembling noticeably, and she put it down and tried to relax with her eyes closed. She felt numb when her name was called and walked stiffly to the doctor's examining room. He was reading someone's chart when she came in, and when he looked up and saw Lisa, he rose and came around his desk to greet her with a slight frown on his face.

"My dear girl, this is a surprise to see you here alone. What seems to be the trouble?"

"Oh, Ivan Petrovich, I first must ask if you can promise to keep what I tell you in complete secrecy, and never let anyone know that I was here, nor why I came to see you ... Please!"

"Lisochka, I'm a doctor, remember? We don't divulge our patients' problems to anyone, so be free to tell me what is bothering you."

Unable to look at Dr. Semenov, Lisa clenched her hands and lowered her head. "Ivan Petrovich, I was in the American Consulate at a party and I drank so much that I don't remember too much about what happened, but for several days now I am nauseated and throw up in the morning. Please tell me if my suspicion is correct?"

"Go behind this screen and I'll have my nurse get you ready for the exam."

Lisa was relieved to escape the doctor's scrutiny and obeyed his orders. When he was through and left her to the nurse to help her get dressed and come out to the room where the doctor was waiting for her, she could tell immediately from the look on his face that he would confirm her fears.

"I'll need a few days for the test to come back with a definite answer, but my preliminary exam tells me that you are indeed expecting. I have to know who the father is and does he know this?"

"No! It's the Consular Attaché, and I don't want him to know because I'm engaged to someone else now and will have the child born as his son. No one is to know the truth except me and you, Ivan Petrovich. PLEASE!"

"The true facts will remain with me in this office, but have you considered the fact that your child will be born as an American citizen if its father marries you right away? By withholding the truth, you will be depriving the child of its rightful citizenship."

Lisa lowered her gaze. "I know, but there are extenuating circumstances, Ivan Petrovich, that deal with my father, and I really can't go into them. I repeat, no one must ever know except you …"

The doctor shook his head disapprovingly. " I'll let you know the result of the test.

Lisa left the doctor's office, gathering her disobedient thoughts into necessary priorities. She calculated there was just enough time to organize a wedding and marry Anton before she started showing. The problem would be later, when she would have to convince him that the baby was premature. "Bless Dr. Semenov, my savior!" she whispered, making a quick sign of the cross. "If Anton won't believe me, he would surely believe Dr. Semenov.

Lisa hurried her steps almost to a run. She would call Anton now and ask him if she could see him early next morning. A few steps from the gate to their house, she stopped. What was she thinking, she thought in dismay, their telephone was hanging in the hallway where everyone could see her and hear what was being said. She turned around and rushed to the skating rink nearby, where she could have some privacy using their telephone in the clubhouse.

Anton's voice sounded unsteady as he asked whether 10 o'clock would be too early for her. Lisa realized that he too was anxious about her decision. Afraid to engage in further dialogue with him over the phone, she said brusquely, "I'll be there," and hung up the receiver on its hook. She ran home, and it wasn't until she was in her room that she realized how rude it was for her to hang up on him. She stretched out on her recliner, closed her eyes, and struggled to calm her racing heart, trying to assess the two future people that lay before her mind's eye.

First, David. What had he been offering her besides a youthful passion and an American citizenship? The language, the people she would meet, the customs, his family, friends, and everything else that would be foreign to her. So absorbed they were with each other's physical attraction that there never seemed to be any wish to delve into the more mundane aspects of life. Now, she could not avoid facing the thoughts of what her daily routine might be like when David would be transferred back to the States. Lisa shuddered at the cold thought that rippled down her back. She would be dependent on her mother-in-law for help, both with minutiae or important problems, and not be self-sufficient for a long time.

Fate had stepped in to offer her an alternative. There was to be a caveat to be sure, in the form of twelve years between her and Anton, and an absence of physical passion. Everything else was familiar and she would have to learn not to call him Uncle anymore. She prayed that her reaction to him would be positive when she would see him in a different way. She dreaded the remaining hours of the day and the agony of anticipation of how she would react the next morning.

The morning dawned windy, disrupted by scraping and catapulting sounds of broken branches and fallen leaves on the sidewalk. While Lisa decided what to wear for her visit to Anton, the wind chased away the clouds and the azure sky greeted her. By the time 10 o'clock approached, Lisa was ready and checked herself one last time using the cheval mirror in her dressing alcove. She told Masha to pin up her luxurious chestnut hair into the fluffed style of the day, making her look sophisticated and older. The white lace collar embraced her neck, and accentuated her tall, slender figure against the dark green dress wrapped tight around her waist. She knew that this early morning at the end of October would not be kind to her uncovered head, but she did not want to hide her hairdo from Anton. Masha, however, begged her to cover her head with an angora shawl. Lisa gave in, realizing how strange it would look wearing a seal coat and no hat.

She was ushered into the guest parlor where Anton rose from an armchair to greet her. Lisa suppressed a gasp. He was clean shaven of his perennial stubble wearing a maroon velvet morning coat with navy quilted lapels. The collar of his white shirt was open and housed a silk print ascot.

She had never seen him dressed that casually, and he not only looked elegant, but years younger. Aware of her surprised look, he raked his fingers through his thick wavy hair and gave her a shy smile. His eyes shone with warmth as he broke the awkward silence by kissing her hand and saying, "Good morning, dear Lisa. I must say, your new hair style is chic and most becoming."

Lisa was tongue tied and the only thing she could think of to say was to comment on his jacket, "I've never seen you in a morning jacket before." She wanted to add that it made him look younger, but stopped herself in time and added lamely, "most becoming."

Anton changed the subject, "Would you like a cup of coffee?"

Grateful for his tact, Lisa nodded, and Anton led her to one of the two loveseats upholstered in forest green silk and facing each other near the fireplace. But instead of sitting down next to her, he chose to sit opposite her in the other loveseat.

"Lisa, my dear," he said, "I don't want to rush you. I know it will take an adjustment for you. I just need to know how you feel about my proposal."

Lisa suppressed a wave of panic. The last thing she needed was to delay the wedding. With great effort she mastered a timid smile and said, "I loved you as an uncle for a long time, and now I have to stop saying 'uncle' and learn to love you as my husband." She dropped her glance with the last words and added, "I don't

NEMESIS | Chapter 3

need extra time for adjustment. Besides, there is poor Papa who can't afford to wait much longer."

With a sigh of relief, Anton moved to her seat, grabbed both her hands and kissed one after the other.

"Oh, my dearest *Lisochka* you have no idea how happy you've made me! I've been in love with you for a long time, waiting for an opportune time to declare myself to you. And now, *golubka*, the rest is up to you!"

Lisa smiled and said shyly, "I thought about our honeymoon possibilities, considering the weather facing us, and thought of Tsingtao. It's on the shore of the sea and should have warmer weather."

Anton burst out laughing. "Oh, you little vixen! I was also thinking of Tsingtao! I'll get to it right away. Well, *golubka*, I'll leave all the other plans for the wedding in your hands."

And so, one of the important parts of planning fell to Anton, while Lisa would be able to give her attention to other matters. At the front door, she hesitated and looked at him with a worried look. "I worry about Papa's excessive concern about the admiral's murder. It's … it seems strange … now that the police are questioning him … they didn't arrest him, just escorted him out."

"I'll look into it. I know someone in the police department, so please leave it in my hands. And by the way, the assassin was quickly apprehended, a Korean nationalist by the name of An Chung-gun who resented Japanese intrusion into domestic affairs, both Chinese and Korean. He was executed for killing the Admiral."

"I'm glad they caught the assassin. Such a misplaced patriotism. What did he expect to achieve by the assassination? Did he have anyone in mind who would take the Admiral's place?"

"This assassin was young and obviously had only one aim in mind, hatred for the Admiral and nothing beyond that."

"I can't understand how the guards missed him getting close to the Admiral and didn't catch him. They must have been sleeping on their feet!"

"The report said the platform was in the dark, and the assassin approached from behind them, so by the time they saw him, it was too late. He may have had a personal vendetta, who knows?"

"Well, I hope Papa won't be hurt while they interrogate him. I'll wait for him at home, and thank you for what you can do."

"I'll do my best!"

All her hope now rested with Anton, and surprisingly, she felt reassured. With a weak smile, Lisa left, and slowly walked home, sorting the recent events with wonder. How fast her life had turned upside down, meteorically making a naïve young girl into a strong woman, plunging her into a tornado of experiences, diversified in substance, and teaching her the value of self-protection. Near the gate to her home, she paused, wondering if the contrary emotions she has been experiencing were over, and whether her monumental secret was truly safe with her. The last hurdle, and the most trying one, was yet to come… David…

Suddenly she thought, *why not see him now at the consulate and get it over with?* Wavering with indecision, she was turning away from the gate. Then, hurrying away from her street, she circled the church, and hailed a parked *droshky* driver to take her to the consulate. As she was driven along the wide Bolshoi Prospekt, she admired the elaborate mansions dotting the street of the wealthy.

Chapter 4

Her father wasn't home yet, and Lisa was able to rummage through her medicine cabinet looking for valerian drops to calm herself.

She should have written David a letter instead of having gone to see him. What a mistake that was!

When he came out from the inner offices to greet her, there was a look of both surprise and pleasure on his face, and before she had a chance of saying anything, he grabbed her hand and pulled her toward his apartment. Although originally, she wanted to remain in one of the empty offices, she had to concede that his choice of the apartment was far more secluded. Once in, he tried to grab her into his arms, but Lisa wiggled out, frowned, and said, "No, David, please don't … I came to tell you …"

David looked at her with a combination of slight frown and smile. "What's the matter? What happened?"

"My father fell into financial troubles and has debts he can't repay. I told you before, that he wanted me to marry someone from our neighborhood, and now one of his wealthy younger friends offered to help him, provided I agree to marry him."

"You mean you're going to sell yourself? And what about us? Leave me just like that, without a thought?" David's voice took on a sharp edge, "What about the plans we talked about? You were so eager to change your father's mind!" He grabbed her by the shoulders and shook her. "Was that just a fantasy?"

"No, David. Don't you understand? It wouldn't solve the problem of his debts. I really don't want to go into details, it is all too complicated." At all costs, Lisa didn't want to tell David about her father's embezzlement and the possibility of going to prison.

"How can you be so detached about our break-up?" David's voice rose in anger, "or was your love only on the surface?"

"David, I spent a lot of time thinking and analyzing our relationship. It was a blinding passion, and I was unwilling to delve into what would await me after we marry and my adjustment to a foreign life. I'm afraid I wouldn't be happy away from Harbin and everything that is dear to me, but most of all abandoning my father who depends so much on me. Please try to understand, especially now when he needs me."

Instead of his understanding nod, she was chilled by the look of icy disgust when he said, "Was it just passion then, and a vision of an American passport that drew you to me? Was there never any real love? How couldn't I see through you! You are nothing but a cheap Russian gold digger looking for the best deal." David forced out a sarcastic laugh. "My mother warned me after I wrote her about you. I almost wrote her a nasty reply. What a fool I've been! It's a good thing I held my temper." His eyes glittered with cold dismissal when he said, "I guess I should consider this a narrow escape from being trapped by a scheming woman!"

In a couple of wide steps, he opened the door, and holding it open, said, "You're free to leave."

Lisa looked at the well-groomed blond hair glistening with pomade that now gave him the look of a distant stranger, and said, "I never coveted your passport because I cherish my own Imperial Russian one, and I must say how glad I am that I shall never have your mother for a mother-in-law!"

She turned and fled his apartment, fuming at his insults, as she hailed a *droshky*. When she approached the house, she yearned for her father to be home.

⌒

Full of anxiety about her father's continued absence, she took the Valerian drops and went downstairs where she paced the floor in the parlor. When Vassili entered the house, she rushed toward him, hugged him, and then asked if he knew who talked about the admiral and the planned reception for him. Vassili shook his head and summoned all the servants into the parlor to question them. They all made the sign of the cross and swore they did not talk to anyone. However, Masha said, "A curious butcher, questioned me why I was buying so much meat and what kind of reception was being planned. I wanted to avoid telling him, but the gossipy butcher insisted, and I was afraid to deny it and start a suspicion, so I told him it was for an important person, but I didn't know the name."

Lisa and her father exchanged meaningful glances and let the servants go about their business. Vassili shook his head. "Needless to say, the police investigator put two and two together and grilled me about the admiral for a long time. Finally, he let me go, especially when Anton showed up and rescued me." Vassili chuckled. "You know my favorite proverb, better have a hundred friends rather than a hundred dollars. Anton told me the money has been replaced in the bank, and that you agreed to marry him. Is that true?"

"Yes, Papa. Anton is a wonderful man and I always liked him. We have to plan the wedding as soon as possible before the winter sets in and prevents us from going on our honeymoon anywhere."

"That's wonderful, *dyetka*, I hope that soon you'll see what an attractive man he is."

"I'm already attracted to him Papa."

"Go ahead with God and do your planning!"

Lisa tiptoed to kiss her father on the cheek and then hurried to her room. There was so much to decide, starting with ordering her wedding dress from her favorite seamstress, and asking Anton to hurry and make reservations for their honeymoon in Tsingtao, where Germans had built a number of European cottages. She had heard a lot about that sea resort and hoped it would be all true. By late afternoon she had important things done, like setting the wedding date in the second half of November in St. Nickolas Cathedral.

And so, after the reservations in Tsingtao had been made by Anton, Lisa was able to give her full attention to other matters. One of which was worrying about her morning sickness which she hoped to be able to hide by staying in bed longer. There was another reason she wanted the wedding to be small and intimate with only a few close friends. The moment word would spread about her wedding, snickering and nasty gossip would circulate among mothers of eligible daughters, that Lisa was selling herself to an older man because he was rich. Never mind that her own father was also rich. She was a spoiled only child and wanted to remain the same. All this was repeated by Masha, until Lisa lost her temper and ordered her maid to keep the gossip to herself. She then grabbed her shawl and dashed out the hallway where, frantic to get out, she shuffled her coats, found her seal one, and throwing her shawl over her head, slammed the door behind her, to run over to Anton's house.

The door started opening at once, but not fast enough for Lisa, so she pushed it in, almost knocking Anton off balance. "Oh, I'm sorry! Where is Agasha?"

"All the servants are in the kitchen. But come in the parlor. Tell me what happened, my darling *Lisochka.*"

Lisa followed him to the parlor but shook her head, refusing to sit down. Instead, she leaned against Anton, wrapped her arms around his neck, and closing her eyes, lifted her face to him with lips slightly apart. The gesture was so obvious that Anton didn't hesitate and touched her lips gently with his. Lisa trembled, clung to him in search of more, and Anton lost control. His gentle touch to her lips exploded into a long awaited, passionate one. The embrace tightened and Lisa felt herself lifted and carried to the couch near the fireplace. "My *golubka*, tell me what happened before I lose total control and regret it later!"

Lisa told him what she had heard from Masha. "Why don't people leave us alone … enjoying gossip!"

Anton laughed. "It's envy, dearest. Envy and anger that I love you and not any one of their eligible daughters. Close your ears and hurry with planning for the wedding. I expected this to happen and that was another reason why I agreed to hurry with the wedding." He kissed her deeply again, and then added, "Besides, it hastened my kiss of which I dreamed for so long!" He stood up. "Now let's laugh this gossip off and start our preparations. Thank goodness there won't too much to do with a smaller wedding."

Chastised and relieved, Lisa went home full of ideas of what to accomplish next.

⏝

The memory of Anton's kiss lingered, and the physical sensation persisted. Lisa worked on the wedding as if in a dreamy fog. There were more things to decide, like making contact with the priest and the ushers.

All the pieces were fitting well. What was left were details of the wedding ceremony itself. The most important of all was asking one of Anton's friends to take her father's place and bring her to church, where he would give the bride away to the groom. Whenever Lisa would ask why parents are not to witness the wedding, she received one word with a shrug, "Tradition!"

She then asked her two closest girlfriends to be her bridesmaids. She felt the number in the wedding party would be sufficient for a small wedding. The two ushers would have the hardest endurance test to their arms, as they would have to hold the church crowns over the heads of the marrying couple, especially over the bride as the priest leads them around *the analoi*, when the usher would have to watch that he didn't step on the bride's wedding dress train and at the same time continue to hold the crown over Lisa's head, high enough not to snag the veil.

The day of the wedding arrived. It was scheduled for three o'clock, and Lisa stood before the cheval mirror in her white silk dress which had a high neckline and long sleeves made out of delicate lace, making her look like a dainty maiden from a Russian fairy tale. Masha was smoothing the folds of the dress and sniffling quietly in accompaniment.

"What's the matter, Masha?" asked Lisa.

"Oh, Barinya, I'm thinking about how it will be in this house without you! I watched you grow up and somehow never thought of you leaving your father's house. Please don't pay attention to silly me. I am happy for you marrying such a wonderful gentleman."

When Lisa was ready, Vassili took her in his new automobile to the church and delivered her to the usher waiting at the entrance to the cathedral.

As soon as Lisa entered the church on the usher's arm, the choir burst forth with an encouraging hymn of, "*Gryadi, gryadi, golubitsa*" {go forth, go forth, sweet dove!} while the usher passed Lisa's hand to the waiting Anton's, who stood resplendent in his silk black tie suit.

The whole ceremony proceeded smoothly and when the rings were exchanged and the couple turned to leave the church, the choir sang a jubilant greeting to the newlyweds.

～

Lisa's father was waiting for the wedding party at his front door, since the dinner festivities always took place at the bride's home. Tears were in Vassili's eyes as he embraced the newlyweds and escorted them to the dining room to the loud calls of *"Gorko! Gorko!"* waiting for Lisa and Anton to kiss to oblige the guests. Lisa giggled because she could never understand why the word gorko — bitter — was used for a kiss, and no one could explain except call it tradition.

Champagne poured freely, calls for *"gorko"* lasted so many times that Vassili finally called it a day, and the guests all shuffled out with repeated wishes of happiness to the couple who had already climbed into the specially decorated white coach harnessed by three white horses. It seemed ridiculous to ride in the *troika* a few yards between the neighbors, so the horses were guided around the block and then stopped in front of Anton's gate.

As they went up the steps to the front door, it opened for them to see the maids, Agasha and Dasha greeting them with freshly baked bread and salt, another tradition of welcoming Lisa into her new home of plenty.

After thanking the servants, Anton led Lisa to the door of her bedroom and turning toward her, said, "I leave you now in Agasha's capable hands. *A bientôt*, my dear." He then kissed Lisa's hand and went to his own bedroom.

Agasha helped Lisa out of her wedding gown and underwear and replaced them with a satin night gown and peignoir. After that, she loosened her elaborate hairdo and thoroughly brushed her hair. Then, leading her toward the bed, she pointed to a narrow piece of sheet, covering the middle of the bed, and said, "Barinya, this piece of cloth covers the sheet and mattress in case it gets soiled during the night. In the morning you may want to pull it out and dispose of it in the laundry basket."

Lisa guessed what Agasha implied, but only nodded and said, "Thank you."

As soon as the maid left, Lisa threw her peignoir off and climbed into bed under the goose down duvet. It wasn't long before she heard Anton's gentle knock on the door and said, "Come in," in a slightly trembling voice. At the foot of the bed, Anton looked at her for a few seconds and then came around to the side, where he took off his maroon silk robe, lifted the duvet, and climbed under it. Then, with his lips on hers, he whispered, "I'll try not to hurt you my darling. I adore you!"

With these words, Anton pressed his mouth into a passionate kiss, and once again a delicious sensation caught her breath and travelled down her belly. Without realizing what she was doing, she responded with equal depth, and at the same time felt his hand caress her with a feathery touch. The next thing she felt were his light kisses showering over her body, and then his mouth entrapped hers again. With it, her mind floated into space, suspended in unimaginable bliss, and yielded to Anton in total submission.

The next morning, when Lisa woke up, Anton was already gone from her bed. She disposed of the piece of sheeting, which she knew would not have any blood, and rang for Agasha who told her that Baryn was at the breakfast table reading the paper and waiting for her. Lisa dressed quickly with Agasha's help and joined Anton who rose from the table with a smile and a loving look. He kissed her hand, and whispered in her ear, "I hope I didn't hurt you too much last night, darling."

Lisa shook her head. "I loved having you near me," she whispered back as well. Anton pulled the chair out for her, and they spent the time over breakfast talking about their honeymoon. Anton had already found several *dachas* for rent and told Lisa that he had engaged one right away and set a date for them to leave as soon as possible.

Still dazed from their wedding night, Lisa listened with a dreamy smile, hardly believing her good fortune.

⌐

Tsingtao proved to be all that they hoped for and then some. The dacha was small and cozy with a fireplace, lace trimmed curtains in the living room. A glassed-in porch offered a view of the emerald sea lapping the sandy shore and soothing one's rattled nerves.

"Aren't you glad I reserved this cottage rather than a suite at a hotel? I'm sure it's well appointed, but still, it wouldn't be as cozy or as private as this, don't you think, *golubka?*"

Lisa smiled. "I can't think of a lovelier place for us than this, dear. Let's walk out and see what is around us."

They walked away from their secluded house to the beach in the cool sunshine, in spite of the late autumn's greeting, and watched the waves break against the formidable cliffs that hugged the German Beach. Close to them was a hotel, competing with a row of cottages curving around the Strand Beach. Lisa savored the peaceful view, free from all gone vacationing families, until she felt her nose tingle from the chilly wind and Anton took her hand and steered her back to their cottage.

Lisa went to sleep at night in Anton's arms, sated with new discoveries in lovemaking.

They stayed in Tsingtao until a proprietary onslaught of snowfall threatened their presence, making their departure on the first available train rapid. The portable chess set helped to pass the time before the chugging of the train lulled them to sleep. When the locomotive puffed to a slow stop at the Harbin station, Anton discovered taxis were not plentiful, but greasing the coolie's hand would have helped, if a Russian coachman with his sleigh would not have interfered. Soon Lisa was pleased to see the familiar gate to her new home, where the loyal Agasha was waiting for them at the door with a broad smile.

Chapter 5

The first morning after arriving at her new home, Lisa woke up with a wave of nausea, and dashed to her private bathroom next to her boudoir. She was so grateful that she and Anton had separate bedrooms. She waited until he left for his office, and then called for an appointment with Dr. Semenov. Her main concern was about the timing of her nausea.

Outside, snowflakes were sliding down the window, reminding her of the slippery sidewalks and the precious cargo she was now carrying within her. She put on her warmest coat, which was a full-length mink and matching hat with ear flaps and muff. She was glad she had recently bought a pair of elegant Bata's fur-lined, non-skid boots. Thus ready, she ventured out to see Dr. Semenov in his clinic which was not far away. Once outside, however, the frost bit her face with unexpected ferocity, and she returned to the house gasping for breath.

Agasha rushed out. "What happened, Barinya?"

"I was going to walk, but it is too cold, so be a dear and call me a *droshky*."

Agasha made a quick curtsy, grabbed her coat and ran out, while Lisa unbuttoned hers and sat down near the front door to wait.

The *droshky* arrived quickly and Lisa was on her way to the clinic.

⌒

After examining her, Dr. Semenov joined her in his office. "You're a lucky girl," he said, "your nausea returned at a believable timing after the wedding. But I can't remain silent every time I see you without reminding you that you'll be giving birth to an American citizen." With a disapproving shake of the head, he sent her home to announce the happy news to Anton.

Dinner was always planned for two o'clock, and she had plenty of time to rest and dress up in one of the new dresses she had bought for her trousseau. This one was made of blue wool, its high-necked collar trimmed in white lace. The wide velvet band hugged her waist and velvet covered buttons ran down from her neckline to her waist completing the outfit. Satisfied with her image in the mirror, she picked up *Anna Karenina* which she had been reading, and settled in the parlor to wait for Anton.

When he came home, Lisa rose and walked toward him with what she hoped was a radiant smile.

Anton stopped. "What a beautiful dress, darling! Are we celebrating something I forgot?"

"You didn't forget anything, but we are celebrating something. Come!"

She took him by the hand and led him to the dining room where two place settings for dinner were waiting for them as usual, except that there was also a bottle of Veuve Clicquot and two goblets.

Anton stared at the table. "What are we celebrating?"

Lisa smiled. "Someone who is already here," she said. "I saw Dr. Semenov today. He told me to get a cradle ready!"

Anton let out an undecipherable, jubilant sound and scooped Lisa into a hug. After a few moments, he released her and sat her down gently in her chair, before sitting down himself. Lisa laughed. "I'm not made of porcelain, darling. I won't break!"

Anton smiled sheepishly. "I'm overwhelmed, *golubka*! I'll have to talk to Dr. Semenov, so we don't make any mistakes while you are in this delicate condition."

A twinge of anxiety cut her breath for a moment. "Go ahead, dear, if that will make you feel better, but I've already got all the instructions from him." She forced a smile and bent over her bowl of borsch, trying to steady her hand. When she raised her head, Anton was smiling and holding his glass of champagne waiting for her to do the same. She joined him and drank hers. After dinner, Anton kissed her, made her promise not to go out in the snow, and left.

Guilty conscience is a real anathema, she thought. *How am I going to live with it from now on? There was nothing to do but to trust Dr. Semenov to assure Anton that everything was normal with my pregnancy and he didn't need to worry.*

Lisa moved to the parlor, sat by the fireplace to keep warm and called the servants in. When they came, she told them her exciting news. Agasha lowered herself to her knees and kissed the hem of Lisa's skirt. "Oh, Barinya, we shall watch over you. Barin must not worry."

Lisa smiled and pulled Agasha off her knees. "Thank you my dear. I feel well and am sure all will go as it should."

But everything did not go as it should. Periodically Lisa spiked a high blood pressure and had to stay in bed on medication for several days at a time. Dr. Semenov warned Anton that he might induce Lisa's labor early due to her condition. The days and weeks dragged on with suffocating dullness, but Lisa endured them without complaint, ascribing that as punishment for her frivolous behavior with David, which she had to hide forever.

When in the doctor's estimation time came, he induced her labor without taking her to the hospital. The labor went on for 10 endless hours of pain, and when at last a healthy looking boy emerged into the bright light and let out a lusty cry, Lisa fell back on her pillows with a smile. The attending nurse took the infant away to clean him up and when she brought him back, Dr. Semenov presented him to Anton, and said, "In another two months, it would have been a larger boy and a more difficult labor. We saved Lisa much pain."

Anton was overjoyed with his fussing son and, after kissing him on his moist forehead, placed him in Lisa's arms.

Lisa smiled weakly, and turning to look at the doctor, whispered to him, "Thank you, thank you!" Then turning to Agasha, gave the baby to her.

Dr. Semenov pulled his surgical gloves off and patted Lisa on her head. "Sleep now, before your son will be back, demanding to be fed."

⸕

They christened him Sergei and called him Serezha. Fortunately, the boy took after his mother with brown expressive eyes and chestnut hair. Lisa tried in vain to keep her son from getting spoiled by the household staff, but his large eyes and fetching smile won out every time. The baby grew plump and healthy, with the exception of expected childhood diseases, which Agasha tended to, now that she had been made Serezha's nanny and kept reminding Lisa that these were necessary to avoid a much more serious form of these diseases in adulthood. Lisa of course knew this, but the yearning to be near Serezha always won over common sense.

Shortly after Serezha's second birthday, Anton came home for dinner late and said to Lisa, "I had to stop at the American

Consulate for some trade business and found the staff attending a celebration after the christening of a newborn girl, daughter of the young attaché, David…something… can't quite remember his last name. I saw the baby as they carried her out. She looks like an albino, so light blond, but then they said both parents are blond. Anyway, sorry I am late. Let's eat."

Bozhe moi! My Serezha has a half-sister! Thank God she is a blonde! Just the same, I hope they will never meet… Lisa opened her napkin and began to eat her cabbage soup, afraid her voice might betray a tremor. Preoccupied with the minutiae of the day, Anton didn't notice Lisa's nervousness, and the meal was consumed in silence. He finished his dinner in a hurry, excused himself right away and left, saying he had a busy afternoon at the office.

Lisa was relieved to digest the disturbing news alone. Actually, she couldn't pin down the reason for her worrisome reaction to this news. David now had a family and she assumed the last thing he would want to unearth would be his affair in the past. She chuckled. How foolish of her to worry!

With that in mind, she went to her drop-leaf desk in her boudoir. She loved its graceful lines. Anton had it painted in black and gold after he purchased it for her from a Chinese artisan downtown. She loved the privacy of its location, and before long was lost in reading and answering notes and letters from her friends.

Time flowed peacefully, Serezha was growing up as a healthy, boisterous boy, making many friends in the neighborhood where Agasha walked him every afternoon. Lisa knew the nanny was vigilant, but still worried because in recent months Chinese bandits, called *hunghuzi*, caused isolated kidnappings of small children and then sold them to childless couples of means. Agasha had become accustomed to Lisa's warnings and understood the young mother's concern.

Typically, on afternoons, Agasha and Serezha enjoyed outings. One sunny day in May, Agasha and Serezha started out toward the HOTKS Club, which had just been transformed from an ice rink to a tennis court. Serezha stopped and peaked through the gaps in the wooden fence, fascinated by the sound of the bouncing balls. Agasha tried to pull him away, but the boy wouldn't move from where he stood.

"Good day, Agasha, let him watch! What's the harm?" Came the voice from her old friend Pelagya pushing a baby buggy.

"Oh! Glad to see you, walk with me."

Agasha glanced at Serezha who had not moved away from the fence, and joined Pasha for half a block, listening eagerly to her gossip.

As they reached the end of the street, she needed to hold Serezha's hand to step off the curb and turned to call him away from the fence.

But he wasn't there. The sidewalk was empty.

Agasha gasped and ran to the HOTKS Club but no one had seen the boy inside. Trying not to panic, she looked at any place within sight. Frantic, her heart in her throat, she ran from one side of the street to another, calling for Serezha, horrified that yet another kidnapping by hunghuzi might have taken place. The thought paralyzed her. She stopped, leaned on a nearby tree … which way had they taken him? …

Pelagya called, "I'll go get his parents," and pushing the buggy, ran to the Platonov's home.

Scared of their reaction, Agasha put her hands to her head. How could she justify her behavior?

"Serezha!!!" she screamed hysterically into the silent void. It was useless. Terrified by what she had done, she started to cover square blocks on the run, calling Serezha to no avail.

Inside Platonov's house, a long, keening wail hung in the air.

Neighbors heard the commotion and ran out to help, well aware that in the past kidnapped children were never found.

Moments later, Lisa and Anton ran out screaming for Serezha. But at the gate, Anton stopped Lisa. "We must wait for the police. Let's go in!'"

Inside, Lisa turned on Anton and pounded his chest with her fists. "Where is he? Go find him … bring Serezha home! Go!"

"The police are on their way, Lisa," Anton said with a trembling voice, "we'll find him."

Police arrived and went to work scouting the neighborhood, all the while aware their efforts were in vain, but doing their job for the parents' sake. The police captain stayed inside to tell them that the hunghuzi never hurt the children.

"They sell them to childless Russian families who take them to their hearts, adopt them, and raise them as their own with much love."

Anton could hardly hold his temper. "We want you to find our child! … Bring him home to us!"

"Oh, my God! Where is he?!" Lisa screamed as she leaned against Anton in a faint.

After the servants lifted Lisa and carried her upstairs where they cared for her tenderly, Anton withdrew to his den, and let the suppressed tears spill out. *My darling, happy boy, where are you now? We have to find you soon! We must!* He whispered through sobbing. After a few minutes, he controlled himself with difficulty, wiped his face, and came out to talk to the police captain.

When Lisa revived, she was inconsolable. Anton, shaking with grief, called for Dr. Semenov's help. The doctor came in a few minutes, listened to Lisa's heart and lungs, and gave her a large dose of Laudanum. He told Anton that because of Lisa's irregular heartbeat, she should be kept from added stress as much as possible.

Concerned for his wife, Anton suppressed his own grief and poured his attention on her. He hired a private detective to keep the file on Serezha's disappearance open, and received the man's reports by telephone, always thorough, and always without any news. Weeks and then months went by without a shred of any encouraging report on the kidnapping. Anton finally dismissed the detective and tended to his wife with loving care.

Lisa held a tangible hope close to her heart, humanizing it by talking to Serezha at night, when the household was asleep. It gave her some measure of comfort, this imaginary world she created for herself and could escape to at will. She prayed every night that Serezha would be adopted by a loving family and told him to be a happy boy with his new parents who would care for him.

Gradually, she regained enough strength to rejoin Anton's hobby of studying trees and their individual characteristics on their property, and then submitted to fate's control of her life.

Chapter 6

Lisa hid her pain as the years crawled by with relentless monotony. She kept Serezha alive in a corner of her soul, which she tapped into. She talked to him in the humming silence of the night. She found it comforting to have devised such a fantasy to fall back on when memories challenged her equanimity. She counted the days and the months as the child grew, picturing how he would look on his birthdays. Times spent with Anton in their garden watching their trees flourish were soothing during the day, but they were short and made her restless.

A quiet time followed until the summer wind from the Gobi Desert in Mongolia delivered its unwelcome yearly sandstorms to Harbin, chasing pedestrians off the streets. Those who could afford to leave the city chose to rent one of the cozy dachas built by farmers who had settled in villages along the Trans-Siberian Railway East and West of Harbin.

When the sandstorms attacked Harbin, Anton and Lisa chose to spend their summer months in Barim, the village along the west side of Harbin and about half-way to the Russian border. They were charmed by it. It was populated by Russian peasants, one of whom rented a two-room cottage to them with a small garden full of blooming bird cherry trees.

On their first morning after arrival, the peasant greeted them with a smile and said, "The sun is shining brightly, and you must see our Matushka Empress Catherine the Great!"

Lisa bit her lip to prevent herself from laughing. The poor man, she thought, must have periodic flights of fancy. She and Anton followed the man into a large clearing where they saw the restive river Yal, gurgling over pebbles clearly visible through the playful water. The peasant, who by that point had identified himself as Mitrofan Petrov, silently pointed his finger at the peak of the far mountain which supported a clearly outlined majestic figure of the crowned queen sitting at the piano. The sun played with the shadows around the body of the granite figure, bringing her to life in an eerie fantasy.

After that morning, Mitrofan became their guide, taking them around and out of the village, into the low hills where the peasants labored over their seasonal work, waving to them with a smile and a deep bow. In the afternoon, after their work had been done, they came down the hills to the pastures where the cows had been grazing and brought them home with their cowbells announcing the end of the day. The villagers welcomed them with a folk song, cheerful enough to uplift Lisa's spirit.

Lisa and Anton cherished that summer in Barim and promised to return in the future.

⤳

Their plans for the summer of 1914 remained unchanged as Anton and Lisa escaped the Gobi sandstorm and settled in Mitrofan's cottage. In the morning, they waved to Matushka Catherine the Great, and ventured into undiscovered virgin wilderness, walking along the playful river, and enjoying the new sights.

In the afternoon, satiated with Barim's surrounding beauty, which they discovered during the morning, Anton and Lisa settled in their tiny garden to relax and enjoy tea with black current jam which they always stirred into the tea instead of sugar. A plate full of freshly baked cookies added to their pleasure. But a few minutes later, Mitrofan showed up on the other side of the gate. "Sorry to disturb you," he said, taking off his hat and bowing.

"Never mind. What's the problem?" Anton asked.

Mitrofan dug into his pants' pocket and pulled out an envelope. "It looked important to me ... I thought maybe you'd want to see it right away." He opened the garden gate and entered to hand Anton the letter with a deep bow Anton recognized at once that the address was written by one of his shareholders at the brewery, the first such letter he had received in Barim. He knew at once, with a sinking feeling, that it carried distressing news because he had left instructions to write him only in emergency.

The shock of the letter's content outweighed any fears Anton may have had. It had a brief note from the shareholder apologizing for disturbing him, and a clipping from the Harbin newspaper. In mammoth black letterhead, the words screamed from the front page that Archduke Ferdinand, the heir to the Austrian throne and his wife, were shot on June 28th as they were riding in an open car in Sarajevo, Bosnia.

The article included speculation that pointed an accusing finger toward Serbia, the country that was an ally of Russia. Anton thought of its broader implication and knew they had to return to Harbin immediately.

As Lisa saw her husband's pleasant smile dissolve in a stream of tears spilling down his cheeks, she was stunned by the dramatic change in Anton's reaction. She was about to ask what happened, when he told her of the tragic event and how the fragile peace in Europe might crumble, igniting widespread unrest and possibly wars. Pain churned in Lisa's stomach as she tried to digest what Anton divulged and she knew that no more questions would elicit answers from her husband. She hurried to the cottage to pack while Anton went to get tickets on the next scheduled train to Harbin.

෴

Their train ride was largely accompanied by silence, suppressing their fears and hoping for some alleviating news on their arrival. The railway station loomed in the distance, its outline wavering through the Gobi sandstorm that was unleashing its fury in a frightening sight.

"Get out your largest scarf, Lisa, and wrap it around your head so that only your eyes are visible," Anton said, omitting any endearment to his wife, and watching Lisa obey his order.

"What about you, dear?" asked Lisa with a trembling voice, but Anton had already pulled a large handkerchief and held it against his face, while motioning her to follow him out. The wind had paused long enough for them to hurry inside the building, closing the door behind them. The air inside was stifling but at least free of sand, and they knelt before the icon of St. Nicholas and prayed for a few minutes, before venturing outside and waving down a taxi. The driver struggled to see his way, but at last the gate to their house could be seen through the restless sand.

Agasha opened the front door when she saw Anton and Lisa run toward the house and they were engulfed in their trusted maid's arms without words.

"I have a brush here, and please don't step off the mat so that the sand remains on it. I'll call Dasha to help free you from this awful mess," Agasha said, calling for Dasha, and then turning Lisa around, brushed her back. Dasha appeared from the kitchen and started to brush the sand off Anton. Then she said, "We kept dinner warm for you, so we'll be ready to serve after you change clothes and shower."

How wonderful they both are, thought Lisa, climbing the stairs and nodding to Anton, who turned to his bedroom. Once in her own room, Lisa lowered herself into the tepid water, washing off the remaining bits of sand that still clung to her face. With reluctance she forced herself to climb out of the bathtub and hurriedly got dressed, aware that her patient husband must be waiting for her downstairs.

When she joined Anton in the dining room, Agasha brought in Lisa's favorite *rassolnik* soup that tasted especially piquant from the infusion of cucumbers and herbs. Anton caught her eye in a silent toast with a glass of wine. "We must be relieved to be home at this time, dearest, and see what the news will be tomorrow. I am particularly concerned about what Russia will do now in support of Serbia."

Lisa hurried to contradict him. "Oh, darling, surely they can resolve their differences by negotiations. Our country has great diplomats, let's dwell on positive results." But her superficial words did not sound convincing. After they finished their meal, she called Agasha to remove the dishes and then come to the parlor. They retired there and asked her what rumors the servants had heard floating around.

Agasha shrugged and shook her head. "Some person high in the government in Europe was shot to death and now gossip mongers are blowing everything out of proportion. I try not to pay much attention to it. I hope you will stay out of this sand-storm and remain at home."

Anton and Lisa exchanged silent glances and remained in the parlor, Lisa with Tolstoy's Kreutzer's Sonata, and Anton with the day's newspaper. It filled several pages with gory details of the Archduke's assassination and the quick capture of the assassin, a high school student, hired by Serbian terrorists. Reluctantly, he lowered the newspaper and tried to project the future in his mind. Nothing but trouble materialized. The Tsar, Serbia's ally, would feel obligated to assist her, but in what form? Anton shuddered when a wave of icy ripples invaded his back. Nothing less than military intervention would assuage the Tsar's honor. And then what? He closed his eyes and shook his head to get rid of threatening thoughts.

With firm decision, Anton forced himself to concentrate on his life with Lisa, and the happiness she had brought him over the years, in spite of Serezha's kidnapping. He studied her face, so deeply engrossed in her book, a disobedient curl tickling her cheek which she kept pushing off her face. With a sudden idea, he turned toward her, "Darling, how about a game of chess? It's been quite a while since we played, but you made remarkable progress the last time, remember? It will keep our minds occupied and away from other things."

Lisa lowered her book and looked at her husband with admiration. "Well ... why didn't I think of it," she said with a chuckle, "Depends on how many of the basic moves I have forgotten." She shrugged. "But I love this game and it's worth a try."

Long untouched ivory chess pieces, intricately carved, seemed to be waiting for them on the chess table and as Lisa and Anton settled down opposite each other, the world around them dissolved, and the pawns in the front row came alive under Lisa's fingers. She loved this game, because it depended entirely on the player's skill and not on the luck of dealt cards. Time dispatched the hours into the atmosphere and although she lost most of the pieces to Anton, it didn't matter to Lisa, and they continued to play for hours, until it was time for supper.

After they had eaten, Anton turned on the gramophone and they spent the late hours enjoying the recording of Eugene Onegin's opera before going upstairs to retire. At the door to Lisa's bedroom, Anton kissed her hand gently and whispered, "I'll come to you in a little while."

Lisa smiled. "I'll be waiting."

~

The next morning Lisa overslept and was shocked to see that it was ten o'clock. Agasha told her that Anton had gone to his office and would be home for dinner at the usual two o'clock. The sand whirls of wind continued relentlessly, and no pedestrians were to be seen outside. Lisa resigned herself to wait for her husband and the news he would bring with him. No speculating on what was happening in Russia, and she decided instead to catch up on her correspondence from friends who had scattered around the numerous resorts both east and west of Harbin, where they were spending the summer shying away from the sandstorm.

Hours seemed to crawl at a half-dead pace, sounding a lugubrious chime from an old grandfather clock. Lisa ignored the somber sound and came down to wait for Anton in the parlor. Once there, she set aside Tolstoi's book and replaced it with a lighter novel, *Innocents Abroad*, by Mark Twain.

When Anton came home for dinner, Lisa rushed toward him, but one look at his face told her that the news was not good.

"Russia has started to mobilize, Lisa. I shudder to think what will happen next."

The curt and formal tone of his voice told her more than the words. Anton took her hand and led her to the dining room where they sat down to wait to be served. Agasha brought in their soup and without saying a word, left the room.

"My God, darling, is the Tsar really going to start a war, or is this just a precaution and threat?"

"We shall know soon enough, *golubka*. In the meantime, all we can do is wait and hope that this will turn out to be an isolated incident." Anton was silent for a while as they ate, and then he said, nodding toward the windblown trees, "Noisy wind is no comfort, either. We are incarcerated at home with no respite from the relentless anger of nature. It looks like a burgeoning threat from the Gobi Dessert."

"If Russia goes to war, how is it going to affect us here, in Harbin?"

"Let's not speculate now, before we learn what happens in Europe. China is not involved in the conflict and besides, we are needed to manage our Russo-Chinese railroad."

Lisa listened to her husband talk without much conviction and preferred to remain silent as they retired to their favorite seats in the parlor. Her heart knocked hard, unrestrained in her chest. What was really waiting for them now? She thought without an answer and wondered how they could kill the anxiety permeating the room. Looking aimlessly around, her glance fell across the parlor on the exquisite chess pieces, their grace and patience waiting for her to join them to continue the game they had not finished the night before.

At first, Anton was surprised, but quickly saw the benefit Lisa was offering him, and joined her. She had learned from the day before, how to store a couple of moves in her memory, and this time concentrated on memorizing a possible third one, highly pleased with herself. The lazy hours came alive, picked up speed, and raced past them. When Anton narrowly won the game, they were both surprised to see that again, like the day before, it was time for supper. Lisa smiled. "I gave you a little harder time today than yesterday, dearest, but even though I lost, I enjoyed the struggle. What do you say if we play every day?"

Anton laughed. "Well, I see that it got under your skin, *golubka*, and all will depend on our situation, the sandstorm duration, what Russia will do, as well as other countries, and how it all will affect us. I know I told you that Harbin won't be changed in any way, but the more I think of it, the less sure I am of what the future holds in store for us. The best we can do is to live a day at a time and not try to guess ahead. Chess of course, will always be at our disposal, provided nothing unexpected happens in the meantime. Now, I see that our supper is ready. We must eat and afterward, let's catch up on our reading before bedtime and try not to think of what's happening in Europe."

Lisa shivered as she listened to her husband, and all her contentment vanished to be replaced by fear of what was going to happen in Harbin.

⌒

They resigned themselves to waiting for news that came sporadically, each more ominous than the last. War quickly widened soon after Russia mobilized. Anton came home for dinner looking pale and stressed. "Germany declared war on Russia," he said in a hoarse voice, cleared his throat, and then added dejectedly, "followed by France. And then Austria's Vienna used Sarajevo as an excuse to do the same. I only hope that our army is well trained and equipped to face such an onslaught."

"What makes you doubt our army?"

"They didn't have much time to get ready..."

A chill ran down Lisa's back. She had always been seeking Anton's optimistic words, but that was a realistic statement.

By the time the end of August came, and Harbin cleansed itself from the sand demon, Europe was on fire.

Russians had fallen into the habit of calling themselves *Harbintsi* and Lisa and Anton hoped to be isolated from the war. "Newspapers tend to exaggerate dramatic events," Anton tried to console Lisa, but his voice lacked assurance, and instead of calming, it frightened her more. As time went on, she finally tucked away her worry into the hidden pocket in her memory and avidly listened to all friends, hugging with firm conviction every welcome word they uttered.

In the meantime, loud unrest among the Russian Army soldiers started to call for the end of war. Increasing numbers of them had deserted, either hiding in their villages, or joining the Bolshevik Communist mobs that rioted and shouted for doing away with royalty and aristocracy.

Anton spread his arms and hugged Lisa. "My dear one, I am so very sorry it's turning out this way!"

Lisa backed away from his arms and turned away to hide her fear. "Thank you, my darling," she said, "for all your kind words."

⌒

Sadly, however, in 1916, facing the growing revolution, the Tsar abdicated, leaving the Provisional Government in his place. He was arrested and with his whole family exiled to Tobolsk and later transferred to Ekaterinburg, farther in Siberia.

During the next year, Anton and Lisa were still clinging to their fading hope that the Tsar and his family would be released, but the news came that the revolution continued to rage over Russia. A middle-class communist, Vladimir Lenin, the head of his Bolshevik Party, took control of the country in April of 1917.

"Who is this man?" Lisa said in anger, "how dare he replace our wonderful Tsar?"

Pale and stooped from all the stress, Anton put his arms around his wife and said, "My dear *golubka*, we must accept the fact that our country is now under control of communism, and the royal House of Romanovs has ceased to exist. All we hope is that Lenin will allow the arrested royalty to leave Russia and be accepted as exiles in some friendly country."

But a year later, in July of 1918, *Harbintsi* read in the newspaper that the Tsar, his family, and many aristocrats were executed in Ekaterinburg. The newspaper gave no details, and such brief notice only magnified everyone's conviction that from then on, all news was censored by the new communist regime. Lisa became hysterical. Although Anton tried to calm her, his own escaping tears got in the way. It took Valerian drops to calm Lisa, who looked at her husband and saw his distraught face.

"There's nothing we can do, darling," Lisa said with a breaking voice. "Let's go to church and pray for their souls."

The brevity of the terse newspaper announcement spoke volumes and Anton and Lisa agonized over the brutal killing. They couldn't stop wondering whether the local officials in Ekaterinburg had decided to take things into their own hands, or had the order come directly from Lenin himself.

"We'll pray with others, my *golubka*, and then cope with our grief in private," Anton said, making a motion for her to follow him.

The church was full of weeping parishioners attending the beginning of *Panihida*, the funeral service for the martyred Tsar and his family. Lisa held Anton's hand and they joined the grieving people in prayer.

At the end of the service, they walked home in silence. Spoken words no longer held any healing for their fractured motherland until Anton said, "We are now no longer subjects of the Imperial Russia and have become refugees. We must wait for what Lenin will offer us instead." Anton said half-heartedly to Lisa, "And the only solace we have right now is the knowledge that we are *harbintsi* and not directly under the communist rule of Lenin." After a short pause, he added, "Lisa, darling, why don't we go for a stroll in *Pitomnik* before dinner? We can try to soothe our nerves among the multi-colored flowers. We both need quiet surroundings and can try to relax on one of their benches."

Anton's suggestion worked magic, and although their sadness remained with them, the silence in the *Pitomnik* became their refuge. Lisa, however, couldn't help but think how shameful it had become to go from being proud citizens of their glorious Imperial Russia, to becoming stateless with no protection from anyone.

Their defunct Imperial passports continued to remain hidden in the safe of Anton's den, as cherished relics of their past.

Thirteen Years Later

Chapter 7

Harbin

1931

Ever since Serezha was kidnapped and Lisa heard *hunghuzi* mentioned, she changed the subject and hid the kidnapping it implied behind the debris of unwanted memories. Instead, she continued to create a loving pair of adoptive parents and a happy life surrounding her son, who was not weeping for his native parents. She ignored the glaring fact that she was paying a high price for her good health. For several months now, she had endured irregular heartbeats causing her to cough spontaneously and draw Anton's suggestion to see Dr. Semenov, but she always refused.

When missing Serezha would become too painful for him, Anton would spend time behind closed doors for as long as he needed. Over the years since the kidnapping, the need to closet himself in his den grew more and more rare.

The adjustment to being refugees had been psychologically difficult as well. The Russian Consulate had been replaced by a Russian Emigrant Committee that registered all resident *harbintzi,* giving them whatever assistance it could. After Lenin had been well entrenched as the Soviet Communist Leader, he made the offer for *harbintzi* to become Soviet citizens. Those who declined, were to remain as refugees without permission to enter Russia. Anton and Lisa grieved in silence. For them, there was no alternative but to stay in Harbin and apply for a visa to some other country. But they found that refugees without a passport needed a sponsor in that country to vouch for them before granting a visa.

"So, nobody wants us," whispered Lisa to herself, but Anton heard her and took her into his arms.

"Darling, have patience, things may change with time."

Things indeed had changed, but not for the best. Japan invaded China with muffled rumors of the sweeping Japanese forces advancing north, and in February of 1932, they occupied Harbin with minimal resistance in the section of Modyagow, followed by trucks full of Japanese soldiers rolling through the rest of the city to their planned encampment.

In the summer, downtown Harbin was flooded by the Sungari River. Chinese men in rowboats offered transportation along the main streets, while crowds of fleeing people fought uphill for shelter and food. The Platonovs were safe uptown, and joined their servants to help the unfortunate residents with food and clothing. The sight of the terror-stricken people would stay in Lisa's memory for a long time.

After the flood receded and people were able to return downtown, Lisa and Anton, overwhelmed and shocked by the deluge, went home to their parlor, where they stood hugging each other in grateful silence of what they had been spared. When time came to retire, Lisa slid down to her knees against her bed and prayed. The ancient Slavonic words seemed to float out of her mouth by someone else's voice, until exhaustion took over and Lisa climbed into bed overcome by slumber.

In June of 1933 Anton told Lisa they should accept an invitation they received to the reception at the American Consulate.

"I really don't feel like going," Lisa said, shaking her head.

For the first time in their marriage, Anton lost his temper. "Enough is enough, Lisa. After all these years, I've run out of excuses. Rumor has it that all the heads of large businesses are being invited and I don't want to be the only one missing. I'm sure this will be a large reception, and we'll be able to slip away early, unnoticed." Anton paused and looked at Lisa with narrowed eyes, "Or is there another reason why you don't want to go to the consulate?"

Lisa looked at Anton and saw a tired face with checkered lines of stress. Suddenly, a wave of hot shame threatened to drown her. She took a deep breath and coming up to him, wrapped her arms around his neck. "Oh, no, dear. I'm just afraid of large crowds, and all the questions I might be getting from people. But you're right, we must go to the consulate."

Anton's face was illuminated by a glowing smile and he whirled her around the room. We'll dance to the Blue Danube waltz. We did it so gracefully years ago, remember?"

Lisa emitted a small laugh, and after giving Anton a breathy kiss, hurried to her room to see what to wear for the reception.

The American Consulate was brightly lit by sparkling chandeliers when Anton and Lisa arrived. They were met with a dazzling array of women in beautiful gowns, men in tuxedoes, and a variety of men in dress uniforms.

This being the month of June, the weather was lenient to the graduating high school girls since this was the traditional White Ball where all the graduating females had to appear in white, competing in elegance with their gowns. They glided on the highly polished dance floor, obviously enjoying the breeze drifting through the open French doors. On one wall, a bright light illuminated the portrait of the newly elected President Franklin D. Roosevelt encased in a heavy, mahogany gild-edged frame. A few tapestries vied for attention with a number of portraits of generals and admirals of WWI.

This year especially, everyone was in their best outfits because one of the graduating students was the daughter of the consulate's staff people, and the Consul General graciously offered to have the traditional White Ball included in the reception. Lisa and Anton of course were not aware of that as they entered the building with smiles, impressed, as usual, by the opulence of the surroundings.

The Consul and his stout wife in a purple satin gown, greeted them at the door and introduced them to the adjutant, who offered them a glass of champagne each and guided them to the ballroom. The glitter of color from the varied gowns dotted with young graduates' white gowns was blinding. The band was playing a waltz, and Anton scooped Lisa in his arms before she had time to react and whirled her around in step with the rhythm of the waltz.

When the dance was over, they walked over to where they could sit down, and then looked around the room for familiar faces. Across the dance floor, a group of other guests were sitting down or standing around chatting. One of them, a tall blond man in formal outfit, was staring at Lisa with a touch of a smile. Next to him stood a rather pretty woman with short blond hair, and next to her stood a young girl with flaxen hair, dressed in a bouffant white dress, obviously one of the graduates.

While Lisa fought to control her accelerating palpitation as recognition settled in, the parents and their daughter walked over, and introduced themselves.

"I am David Jones, this is my wife, Jane, and this is our darling daughter, Nancy." He bent over Lisa's hand in the facsimile of kissing it, which she offered him with a superhuman effort to keep it from trembling, and wondered what he would say next, after he shook Anton's hand.

"We met before, when I was a new attaché here, and Lisa taught me a few Russian words, which I'm afraid I have already forgotten. I must say, Lisa, the past years were kind to you."

Vastly relieved, Lisa smiled and asked, "What position do you hold this time?"

"I'm the consulate's secretary. I'm happy to be back, because I remembered Harbin's beautiful environment and the lovely summer resorts east and west of it." David looked at his wife and daughter. "Fortunately, we all love it here." They both nodded, and Lisa, turning her attention to his daughter, said, "You look lovely, Miss Nancy. I'm sure you're eager to go for the ride in the rowboat on the *Sungari?* I'll never forget my own ride after the White Ball. It looked to me then as if the river was dotted with gardenias floating downriver with the current."

They exchanged a few more banal sentences and the Jones family left them. Lisa felt it was prudent to compose herself outside the ballroom and excused herself in search of the lady's powder room. Luckily, it was close by and empty. Glad to be alone, she leaned over the sink holding onto it with both hands, took several deep breaths to calm herself, and then looked in the mirror. She put on a touch of lipstick, picked up her beaded purse, and then turned to leave, but the door flew open, and Jane Jones strode in shutting it behind her.

Her face with narrowed gray eyes and thin lips was distorted by a disdainful look.

"I know all about your affair with my husband. He told me how relieved he was when his involvement with you ended. I don't want a scandal here, but if you have any desire to contact David and cheat on your older husband," here Jane paused to sneer, "I can assure you, I won't hesitate to expose you!"

Lisa was shaken. No one had ever spoken to her like that. Holding onto her dignity, she said in an icy voice, "I won't deign to reply to this," and tried to pass Jane, but the woman turned and left the powder room in front of Lisa, slamming the door.

The implication was ominous, and she feared that Jane would carry out her threat, given the slightest suspicion. The woman can sleep well, Lisa thought, no scandal would ever be necessary. In fact, if Jane knew how protective Lisa was of Anton, no scandal would ever take place.

⤳

On the way home, Anton asked Lisa, "Well, dear, it wasn't so bad, was it? I saw Mrs. Jones go to the powder room after you. Did she speak to you?"

"Just some. Unpleasant woman."

"Well, at least you enjoyed dancing, darling."

The rest of the ride home was in silence with Lisa leaning her head on Anton's shoulder.

At home, after Agasha helped her get ready for bed, Lisa said, "Agasha, you're getting on in years and I sometimes think you can read my mind. I don't know how I could get along without you!"

"I hope to be with you till the day I die. After all, I'm only seventeen years older than you," Agasha said, curtsying with a quiet good night.

Lisa waited until the maid left, then threw her duvet off and tiptoed to Anton's door.

"Darling, are you decent?" she whispered, and when he opened the connecting door, dressed in pajamas and a silk, maroon robe, she kissed him and said, "I'll wait for you to join me when you are ready."

The next morning, Lisa stretched luxuriously on awakening and relived in her mind the night of love, being in Anton's arms, enjoying his intimate caresses with abandon. Although his loving had been frequent over the years, this one had freed her of her reserve, and lifted her from the burden of grief that hung around her shoulders.

After breakfast, Anton led her firmly to the parlor, where he sat her down next to himself on the loveseat, took her hands in his, and said, "My sweet *golubka*, I watched over the years how you coped with our loss of Serezha and was saddened to see you wrapped in your grief. The upheaval in our country, the revolution's frightful fratricide, the communist takeover, the slaughter of royalty, all that had added to your distress. I too grieved, but in privacy, trying to give you support, but you continued to stay in a cocoon of despair and wallowed in it. This reception yesterday broke your mold of privacy and I hope I have my old *golubka* back again." Anton choked on the last few words and sat back, releasing Lisa's hands.

Nothing upset Lisa more than the realization that Anton's suffering had been as great as hers. The subconscious awareness that Serezha was not his son made her realize how selfish she had been the last twenty years by not reminding herself that her husband believed that Serezha was truly his child as well.

Serezha must be with a loving family she must not seek him and throw the other family into upheaval with her egotistical pursuit. She should concentrate instead on making it up to Anton by grieving together with him. She had to concentrate now on joining him wherever he would want her to go and do it willingly.

Chapter 8

In anticipation of the next Gobi sandstorm, Anton and Lisa chose Handaohedzi on the Eastern side of Harbin, farther from the Gobi Desert than the Western side and moved into a rented dacha from a welcoming villager, Ivan Shubov. His family consisted of a well-nourished wife Anna and two grown sons, Oleg and Igor. Both sons were tall, muscular, and blond. Lisa exchanged surprised glances with Anton, for the two young men carried the names of historic warriors who fought for the fatherland, and not the common peasants' names, such as Ossip or Matvei, etc.

After introducing his sons, and having caught his new tenants' meaningful glances, Ivan chuckled and said, "Our boys were born in Manchuria, and we wanted to be sure they never forgot their country's history."

Duly impressed by such a unique expression of patriotism, Lisa and Anton enjoyed their simple life in the village, watching the sons taking turns milking the cow, or helping their mother pluck the chickens for dinner. The abundance of picket fences reminded them of villages in Russia they had seen in paintings. Handaohedzi was a spectacular settlement, with an open square in the center surrounded by *izbas* ending at the base of a hill where a dirt road led up to the pharmacy, staffed by a young Russian pharmacist. Her name was Inna Trofimova, and she had many stories to tell Lisa, who visited the pharmacy and discovered a clinic attached to it. One of the stories Inna told was about the village women who were not shy to lift their skirts and use their hands to point to the area that needed attention.

When Lisa asked how she handled this, Inna replied, "I quickly pulled their skirts down and took them to the clinic for some privacy."

Lisa and Inna laughed. "I'm sure they didn't teach you all this in school!" Lisa said, shaking her head through her laughing spell. Giving Inna a spontaneous hug, Lisa left the building and started down the steep hill. Walking in her high heels was much more difficult than going up, and Lisa began to laugh at her own city outfits and how funny she must have looked as her downward trek increased in speed, and before she knew it, she was sliding the last few yards, sitting down on the sandy path.

At the bottom, two smiling and sturdy villagers helped her up and asked if she was hurt in any way, but Lisa chose to make fun out of the incident and said, "Next time I shall wear proper clothes and shoes." The men spread their arms. "Our country folk are always facing challenges from nature!"

Lisa shook the bottom of her skirt and stood, admiring the scenery. All around her were trees, spruce, firs, birches, aspens, shading the square from the hot sun where children frolicked unsupervised. The traffic consisted of an occasional horse-drawn cart, its slow-moving horse's hoofs and squeaking wheels giving plenty of time to alert the children to let the cart go by. There was no sign of Japanese occupation, another unexpected attraction. Such bucolic scenes and easy access to medical help charmed Lisa and Anton and they decided this village would be their yearly escape from the dust storms. When wind-blown golden and burnished brown leaves crunched under their feet, announcing an advent of autumn, Lisa and Anton knew it was time to return to Harbin.

They thanked Ivan and his family and boarded the train. The ride to Harbin was uneventful, but when the taxi drove them home, Lisa noticed an absence of pedestrians on the sidewalks, and the empty streets where usually Chinese tradesmen peddled their wares in their singsong voices. The eerie silence bothered Lisa, but she kept her concern to herself, aware that Anton was watching the street as well.

When Agasha greeted them at the door, she had such obvious fear on her face that both Lisa and Anton were surprised. "Agasha, what happened?" asked Lisa and led her into the parlor to explain. The maid covered her mouth with her hand for a moment and then said, "Oh, you haven't heard? The American Consulate is closed because their Secretary's daughter was kidnapped by *hunhuzi* a week ago, and so far we don't know the details because they are keeping it all out of the newspaper. They even have a padlock on their gate."

Lisa and Anton were speechless, and when Agasha left the room with a quick curtsey, they went to the loveseat by the fireplace. For a few minutes both sat in silence absorbing the news. With her vivid imagination, Lisa thought how heart wrenching it must be to have a grown daughter in the hands of the bandits. Although she had suffered all these years, consoling herself that a lack of ransom was proof that Serezha was with a loving family who cherished him, she shuddered now, the pain of losing Serezha surfacing, raw and fresh.

Chill crawled down her spine as her thoughts returned to Nancy. What must be going through Jane's mind picturing her daughter in the hands of the kidnappers, whoever they were? Lisa rose and turned to Anton. "Dear, I have to go to my room for a while and when you come home from the office, we'll talk." Anton nodded and Lisa left.

Once in her room, she looked down the street, where the fallen leaves swirled into a funnel by gusts of wind. Again, her thoughts went back to her own grief and how she had craved to have another woman who could have had given her empathy but there had been nobody. In Jane's case, however, there was one… Without allowing herself to speculate any longer, Lisa grabbed her angora shawl and told Agasha to call for a taxi.

∽

The gate to the consulate was locked and an American military guard paced behind it. Lisa got out of the taxi and handing the guard her calling card, through the slats of the gate, said: "I'm a friend of Mr. Secretary and his wife."

The guard took her card and went to the front door where he handed the card to the doorman with a few words. In a few minutes the man returned and with a shaking head, said a few words to the guard. Lisa had never been so summarily rejected. She grabbed the gate lock and shaking it slightly, said to the guard in a firm voice, "Tell Mrs. Jones that I have an important message for her."

The doorman disappeared again, and Lisa waited. When he returned with a shaking head again, he said, "Mr. Jones said that his wife doesn't feel well enough to receive visitors."

More than ever determined to get through, Lisa took a deep breath and said, "Please! Tell her I have gone through the same agony and want to share something with her that may help." Lisa swallowed the humiliation of having to disclose to the doorman the real purpose of her visit. She grabbed the iron slats of the gate to show that she was not about to leave.

This time the wait was short and David Jones himself showed up. He looked haggard with sunken eyes and pale face.

"I'm sorry, Lisa, for having you waiting. Please follow me."

They walked to the back of the consulate in silence, where the rental places were across a well-kept garden. David unlocked the door, showed Lisa in, and locked the door after her. Noticing her surprised look, he shrugged and said, "There's little to do for American families here except to depend on one another, especially those with little children. They yearn for any scrap of information that they can pass on to their neighbors. So, please, let's go into the living room and I shall call Jane to join us."

When he left her, Lisa looked around the room. It was furnished in traditional Victorian style of mahogany wood chairs and overstuffed sofa. Two loveseats were facing each other near the fireplace. Then her glance rested on the bookshelf full of family photographs. Many spaces were empty, leaving clear imprints of various sizes of frames. Lisa's hands tightened at the realization of what was removed and why.

The door opened and Jane entered, holding on to David's arm. Lisa took a step forward trying hard to hide her reaction to the look of devastation on Jane's face. She didn't seem to care or even been aware of the tears still trickling down her face, her reddened eyes and no lipstick.

Lisa suppressed the venomous words Jane threw at her during the ball. She had to restrain herself from rushing toward Jane and putting her arms around her. Her impulse was interrupted by David who clearly planned to remain by his wife's side and was about to sit down. This would have ruined Lisa's intention and she wanted to have her way. "David, I don't mean to be rude, but what I came to share with Jane, belongs to two women who are grieving."

The last word made David stop and look at Lisa with a searching look. She gave him a pleading look in return, and David walked out. As soon as the door was closed, Lisa sat down next to Jane on the loveseat and took her hands in hers. Jane must have understood Lisa's good intentions and let out a flood of fresh tears.

"The kidnappings are rampant now," Lisa began, "and they are done by the local *hunghuzi* who are after the money alone, and it's not in their interest to hurt the victims. All they want is to frighten the parents into paying the ransom, after which they will return your daughter. Believe me, I know..."

"How do you know?" Jane asked with a trembling voice.

"Because they stole my son — my only child."

"Oh, dear! What happened? Was your son hurt?"

"At the time, he was two years old and we never saw him again, but I came to..." a deluge of tears flooded Jane's face before Lisa was able to finish her sentence.

"Please, please hear me out. Things are not as bad as you think. Please let me explain!" Lisa pleaded while holding Jane's hands, and proceeded to tell her the painful details of Serezha's kidnapping. "Before going to sleep at night, I created in my mind an image of my son looking well and talked to him as though he was near me. It helped to get through the early years. I still do it on occasion."

Jane's pained facial expression spoke volumes as she leaned forward and nodded. "Please forgive my behavior in the past, but I still don't know what will happen to Nancy."

"I'm sure the *hunhuzi* will send you a ransom demand any day now and once you pay it, Nancy will be released. They have their own code of honor, and it's not in their interest to hurt her."

Jane patted her face with her handkerchief and rose. "Thank you for giving me hope ... it was kind of you to share all that with me." As she walked with Lisa to the door, she said, "Please forgive me again. I was jealous. Now I see there was no need to feel that way."

Lisa gave the distraught woman a hug, then stopped at the door. "Be sure not to wait too long after you get anything from the kidnappers. Accept their demands even if you need time to collect the amount of ransom, so they know that you plan to pay."

Lisa picked up her shawl and was about to leave, when Jane grabbed her hand and said, "Oh please, come back soon. We can have coffee in the mid-morning or tea in the afternoon. Just your presence here, with me, helps! Can you understand that?"

"Of course I do, Jane. You can count on me. Just have David leave the order at the gate to always let me in." Lisa smiled and left, closing the door behind her gently.

Chapter 9

Lisa returned home satisfied with what she had set out to do. From now on, there was nothing to do but wait for the ransom note. When Anton came home for dinner at two o'clock, Lisa greeted him without preamble by telling him what she had done that morning.

Speechless for a few moments, Anton moved toward his wife and gently put his hands on her cheeks. "Darling, I'm at a loss for words... So proud of what you've done! Now tell me all the details of what happened, the state of mind of the unfortunate couple, and how are they doing. Tell me everything."

Lisa described everything about her visit to the Jones' apartment. The only thing she withheld from Anton was the short exchange of words between her and David while they were crossing from the offices to the resident apartment building. She hoped that Anton wouldn't ask about the sensitive past, and he hadn't.

"I'm vastly relieved to see you break out of your shell of grief, my darling, and very proud of what you achieved. I'm only disappointed that you didn't consult with me first."

"I thought about it and wanted to have your support but was afraid you'd object to my going there alone. But the whole purpose of this visit was a woman to woman emotional exchange."

"Of course, *golubka*" Anton paced, then turned to Lisa. "It's just my male ego feeling left out of something you were doing important without my participation. But of course, you were right in supporting Jane alone. You've made a giant step out of your shell of grief by sharing your own tragedy with another grieving woman. Do visit her as often as she wants you. Needless to say, we must not forget her husband too, and that is where I come in as another grieving husband."

Lisa caught her breath. That was the last thing she wanted to happen. She didn't know what to say without arousing his suspicion. Before she found her power of speech, Anton pointed to the Chinese escritoire gracing the corner of their parlor and said, "I'll write him a letter and share with him my emotional experience in controlling my grief."

Lisa felt his warm lips on her forehead as he said, "I have an idea, *golubka*, let's take a taxi to the *Pitomnik* and take a leisurely walk. Harbin is proud of its city garden and we have yet to visit it this year. The fragrance of the blooming flowers should be soothing. Your favorite, lily-of-the-valley, is not out yet, but others will be out in abundance. What do you say, hmm?"

"Oh, I'd love to go for a walk there. What a wonderful idea!"

The taxi dropped them off at the entrance to the *Pitomnik*, and Anton told the driver to come back in an hour. They walked in and immediately were overwhelmed by the variety of color greeting them of blooming flowers. As they went deeper into the garden, other blossoms greeted them in abundance, some drifting off the trees and covering the sand of their pathway. After a while, a sudden breeze played with the leaves around Lisa's feet, raising them over her shoes, tickling her ankles and making her laugh.

"What's so funny, *golubka?*"

"I feel so good for the first time in ages! It's beautiful here, and the weather is smiling at us. You know, I actually hate to leave this little paradise."

Anton smiled. "We can come here every day if you like."

The air was pure, free of the city dust and human travail, whispering to them through the music of silence. Lisa drew deep drafts of perfumed air and leaned her head on Anton's shoulder. "Darling, you can't imagine how content I am with having come to terms with my life and what it is teaching me." The taxi was waiting for them on the street, and Anton helped Lisa to climb in. As they approached the center of town, Lisa cried out, "Stop, stop, at the corner of Novotorgovaya and Bolshoi Prospekt! They always have buckets of cut flowers for sale over there."

When they returned home laden with bunches of chrysan-themums and carnations, Agasha relieved them of their fragrant flowers, and they settled down in their parlor. Anton picked up the newspaper, and Lisa reclined on her loveseat and closed her eyes to relive the day's events. How gratifying she felt to have had a pro-ductive visit to Jane with a promise that the contact between them would remain open. Poor woman, Lisa thought. Jane was beside herself, imagining all sorts of things the *hunghuzi* were doing to her daughter. If Jane didn't contact her tomorrow, she would call and tell her that she should not hesitate to talk to her anytime she felt like it. Lisa knew the delay in the ransom note was deliberate to prolong the parents' anxiety, and to make them agree to their demands.

In the next couple of days, Jane talked to Lisa through tears, and it was obvious that she was catching every word of explana-tion about the delay from the captors with hunger.

On the third night the ransom note was pushed through the slats of the consulate gate by a phantom man, who slipped away without stirring a whiff of air. But the note that he dropped through scraped the cement as it fell to the ground, making enough sound for the guard to peer from behind the gate, but the placid night did not divulge the secret, and the moon, hiding behind the clouds, offered no help either.

The guard entered the lighted building to read the address, saw the scrawled writing, and knew at once what it was. He debated only a minute whether to wait until morning or wake Mr. Jones now, and decided on the latter. He called another guard to replace him and hurried across the back yard to the housing building. It took a few minutes before David, dressed in pajamas and robe, answered the door.

David grabbed the note with a trembling hand and stopped the guard who started to walk away. "Did you see anyone?"

The guard described the whole scene, bowed and left.

⌒

The phone rang at 9 o'clock in the morning when Anton and Lisa were having breakfast. Agasha answered and moments later came into the dining room. "It's for you, Barinya."

Lisa used all her power of restrain from rushing to the phone, and when she heard Jane's voice teary and garbled, the only words clear enough were a desperate cry, "Please, oh please, come over... as soon as you can!... the ransom note... it came during the night... nobody saw who brought it to the consulate gate... so terrible... come quickly, I'm beside myself, and David doesn't know where to turn for help!"

"Shh, Jane, dear, I'll be there after breakfast. Anton will drop me off on his way to work." Lisa hung up the phone and returned to the dining room telling Anton about it. "The poor woman," he said, "I wonder what the ransom demands. I hope they will find a way to meet it. Go with the Lord and see what you can do. If you think I can help in any way, let me know."

Lisa nodded, and taking the last sip of coffee, followed Anton to the car. The ride was short, and after she waved goodbye to her husband, she ran to the consulate gate, and identified herself. This time the guard let her in right away. Glad that there was a path to the apartments outside the consulate building, Lisa ran over and knocked on the Jones's door. Jane answered, her eyes reddened and puffy. Lisa hugged her and went in. After David came into the parlor and greeted her, Lisa noticed dark circles around his eyes betraying a sleepless night. "I'll let Jane tell you everything, as I have to decide what to do about the ransom." After he left the room, Jane told Lisa that the ransom demanded two thousand U.S dollars to be left at a certain spot in the *Pitomnik*, in the afternoon when most people were at home having dinner. Specific instructions would follow in a week. Jane paced the floor and rubbed her hands. "The trouble is where are we going to get so much money? The Consul General has to obey the original order of not lending money to the staff. My parents are working people and certainly don't have the necessary sum. David's mother is well off, but I doubt if she can get that much money in cash to send us in time to meet the deadline."

"If David is contacting his mother, surely, she will do everything she can to save her granddaughter."

"David is sending a telegram to her right now, but we don't know how long all this will take and we have so little time to do it." Jane's voice broke and she struggled to gain her composure.

Lisa hesitated to embrace Jane, to avoid another outburst of weeping, and gently stroked her distraught friend's hand. "The *hunhuzi* know how much time you need. Be patient, dear. I know how agonizing this is but try to be strong."

Lisa stayed with Jane until David returned from sending the telegram. Jane went to him and he held her close. Lisa quietly excused herself. The waiting, the anticipating of news of any kind would be best done in private.

❧

Jane called Lisa every day, apologizing each time for disturbing her. Lisa always tried to make her feel welcome and listened with patience to the poor woman's sorrow. Near the end of the week, Jane called with the news that David's mother had sent a telegram saying that she would be able to get the money but wasn't sure if it would get to them in time.

When Lisa went there, Jane hugged her and said, "David copied his mother's message and included a note asking for a week's extension. I hope they will agree to wait. David went to leave the note where they said to leave the money."

"It was smart of David to copy his mother's telegram. *The hunhuzi* want the money. I 'm sure they will wait an extra week."

"My poor Nancy, what condition are they keeping her in?" Jane said shaking her head and walking up and down the room.

"It's in their interest to keep her unharmed, Jane dear. I know it's torture to wait." Lisa said, putting her arm around Jane's waist and leading her to a loveseat. "How is David holding up?"

"He's been wonderful to me," Jane said sitting down. "But I can see his swollen eyes, so he can't hide his pain."

"My heart aches for both of you. But remember you told me that Nancy is a strong girl, so I'm sure she can endure the discomfort she's in. I'm sure they won 't harm her while they wait."

"Oh, Lisa, I don't know how I would have survived without you! You've dulled the edge of agony."

Lisa rose to leave. "Hold on to what I told you, Jane, I'll be home all day."

❧

Lisa went home and waited for Anton. When he came home, he said, "I left my letter at the door to the consulate with the guard. I hope it will help David to know how I coped when our son was kidnapped."

Lisa hugged him and sat down in the parlor to reflect on the day's events while waiting for dinner, and what would happen if the money wouldn't come through in time? Tossing ideas in her mind, Lisa faced the last resort possibility that Anton could come up with the necessary sum out of the brewery fund and twist his shareholders arms to agree to a loan. She didn't dare suggest this to Anton who might already have thought of that and been rejected. What other solution could they come up with? Lisa wondered if they had enough money saved in their own bank. There were two more days, and something surely would be resolved.

Chapter 10

During the extended week Jane and David were in agony waiting for the telegram from his mother. For Lisa there was an added fear that over the years the *hunhuzi* had changed the rules of their kidnapping demands and had become less tolerant. Anton tried to divert her on the deadline but with no success.

"How cruel these *hunhuzi* are … don't you see, Anton? We never know what to expect from them."

Anton nodded and led Lisa to the loveseat with a book, which she kept on her knees without reading.

When the week drew close to an end, the phone rang and Jane's voice bubbled with happy words that the money was on the way, and David had gone to leave a copy of the telegram to a designated spot in the *pitomnik*.

Lisa listened with a broad smile.

"Now we have to wait for the detailed instructions when to drop off the money and bring our daughter home," Jane was saying. "In the meantime, I'll be putting all pictures of Nancy back on the shelves where they belong. I'll also have the maid dust and freshen the bedroom with an open door. After that we must plan a homecoming party for our darling daughter!"

"Do you want me there with you when Nancy comes home?" Lisa asked.

"Oh, no, dear friend. Nancy would want total privacy. I hope you understand!"

"Of course, Jane dear, call me anytime you're ready for me."

Lisa hung up the receiver and walked slowly to the window that overlooked their blooming garden. But the usual pleasure of seeing it wasn't there. Jane's happy voice underscored Lisa's lack of hope to see her son ever again. *What happened to the artist's invisible brush to foreshadow the approaching autumn?* Lisa thought in confusion. Hadn't she always loved the autumn colors before?

She paced the parlor for a while, then once again peeked outside. Nature was playing games with her, for the sun was there, helping her to relax, in view of what she should expect to see at the Jones' apartment next time she went there. She hoped that Jane's call would come in late afternoon, when Anton would be home from the office, and they could go together. Yes, she had to re-learn the lesson of patience in anticipation of everything good that the sun's rays were sending down to earth.

Several days went by before the telephone rang, and she almost fell over the antique chair that Anton purchased for her. Running down the stairs, she held her narrow skirt up to her knees, and then breathlessly answered the phone.

"The wind has picked up, Lisa, maybe it's the remnant of the sandstorm," Jane said. "I think we should wait making plans to celebrate Nancy's homecoming until after the weather settles down. In the meantime, we would love to have you and Anton come over for cocktails later this afternoon."

～

Anton and Lisa were on their way to the Jones' apartment, and when they got there, Anton knocked gently on the door.

"Come in, come in," Jane's jubilant voice sounded from inside, and before Lisa could collect her thoughts, she was in Jane's warm embrace, her whisper repeating, "She is home, home!"

As soon as Jane released her, Lisa and Anton said hello to David who had been standing by the door to the dining room. As Lisa set her attention on Nancy, the young girl curtseyed to her and then to Anton, who remained standing next to David, smiling.

After Lisa and Anton greeted Nancy, Jane said, "Please sit down, I'm glad you both were able to come over on such short notice. It's been rather hectic around here and we let the time slip by unnoticed. Nancy is rested now and will tell you of her ordeal."

Then Jane rang for the maid and told her to bring in the cocktails. Nancy came over to Lisa and sat on the chair near her. The blue silk dress matched the young girl's blue eyes, and her blond hair was short and waved in the latest style. Aside from a little pallor, she looked well-groomed.

"We're so happy to see you home," Anton said from across the room.

"Go ahead, dear," Jane prompted Nancy who seemed reticent. "Well... I was walking to visit a friend when suddenly a Chinese man wearing a mask grabbed my hands, twisted them to the back, and as I tried to fight him, he tied my hands together and" ... Nancy stopped and gulped some air ... "he stuffed a rag in my mouth ... it was awful ... two other men appeared and dragged me to a beat-up car and pushed me in ... there was another man inside with a syringe ..." Nancy winced "... he injected me in the arm ... I don't remember anything after that ..."

The young girl shuddered, paused for a while, then went on.

"When I opened my eyes, I was lying on a thick pile of straw, and a bunch of Chinese teenagers were pointing at my skirt and laughing ... they ignored angry shouts from a tall bandit standing at the foot of my bedding with a rifle... his face was rugged and his narrow eyes glared at me. I was terrified ... He barked at me in passable English, that I had no fear of abuse as long as I obeyed his orders and my parents followed their instructions..." Nancy stopped, took in a ragged sigh, then went on. "If I didn't obey his orders, things would be worse for me and they---"

"That's enough!" Interrupted David in a shaky voice, "You've already told us all the details. You don't have to do it again. I'm sure Mr. and Mrs. Platonov got the idea of how it was."

Lisa sensed how painful it was for the parents to hear all this, and turning to David, said, "May I have a glass of sherry, please?"

Jane dabbed her eyes with a handkerchief and turned toward Nancy, but Nancy shook her head, "No, thank you . . . Please, you all enjoy sherry. I would rather have coffee. I missed it so."

Jane called the maid. "Bring coffee and the sweet American rolls from the bakery, the ones we call doughnuts, filled with raspberry and strawberry jam."

When the maid returned and placed everything on the low table in front of them, Nancy savored the coffee and tasted the doughnuts, while the rest sipped the sherry.

As Lisa continued to enjoy the sherry, she suddenly felt pressure in her chest, as though a heavy weight had landed over her heart. The last thing she wanted was the happy family to realize that their daughter's release from captivity was painfully underscoring her life as a mother who had lost her son forever.

As soon as it was polite, Lisa gave a meaningful look to Anton, thanked the Joneses for having invited them, and left.

At home, Lisa dismissed everyone who wanted to help her, ignored Agasha who tried to lead her to the dining room for supper and went in herself, telling Agasha to start serving supper. While waiting, her mounting grief, well controlled for years now, unearthed from the buried grave somewhere in her brain. The pressure in her chest grew into a burgeoning pain and Lisa knew that after supper she had to see the doctor.

Anton scooped his moaning wife in his arms and after placing her in the car, raced to the doctor's office.

The wait, while the doctor was examining Lisa, was agonizing for Anton, and when at last Dr. Semenov emerged, his face had a touch of a smile.

"Not life threatening, just another attack of angina. Be sure she takes the medication I'll prescribe and as long as she takes it, she will be fine. Many people live out their normal lives with it."

They rode home in silence, digesting what had been told to them and Anton was determined to protect Lisa the best he could. He hired a nurse for several hours a day, while Lisa tried to dismiss the danger of what the doctor told her, yet willing to let her basic common sense take charge of her health.

Agasha made sure the nurse had everything she needed for her mistress' comfort.

⌣

Lisa allowed herself one week of rest and then, defying the doctor's orders, accepted the Jones' invitation to high tea in their apartment. Anton tried to object, but Lisa told him that she didn't want to give in to health weakness, as it would only aggravate her emotional shakiness. Besides, she argued, Jane told her they were eager to protect their position, wanting to avoid unavoidable questions from well-meaning but curious guests, and trusted only a few invited friends.

As it turned out, the gathering for a festive tea was small, five couples who talked about the rumors of the growing power of the Japanese forces and how imperative it was to avoid any confrontation with them. Everyone said they were glad to see the young girl looking so well and nothing was asked about her ordeal. The time went fast, and when Lisa and Anton left, he suggested they have supper downtown, but Lisa declined. "I've had a long day, dearest, and look forward to keeping the positive memories floating in my mind at home."

Anton said, "and we should be flattered they included us in their small circle of friends. I'm glad we have them added to the circle of our own Russians. It will be nice to broaden our circle of friends, especially the young ones who bring fresh air, so to speak, into our lives. We may learn things about cities abroad, also about Americans' daily lives."

Lisa nodded and gathered enthusiasm about what the future may now offer them in their expanded circle of friends. She was sure that fate drew her into the Jones' lives and their near tragic loss, to let her assess her own life and the grace that fate bestowed upon her.

Chapter 11

Time tiptoed for Lisa. Life had settled into a quiet routine and she waited for the change of seasons. The cracks of cobblestoned streets harbored the autumn dirt, which splashed on pedestrians' boots causing them to come up with choice expletives. One morning the heavens opened and sifted the crystalline snowflakes on the weary earth, covering the same dusty cobblestones with an untampered white blanket.

The first winter after Nancy's kidnapping slipped by and spring's floral fragrance drew people to *pitomnik* to enjoy their favorite flowers. Lisa prepared for their annual summer escape from the Gobi sandstorm. As usual, they went to Handaohedzi where the Shubov family's rental rooms waited for them. This time, only Oleg and Igor welcomed them and brought in their luggage.

"Our parents are out distributing produce and milk to our customers," volunteered Oleg, and turned to leave the room, pulling at Igor's shirt to follow him, but Anton stopped him. "Maybe it's just as well they are not here right now, because I want to talk to you about another matter." Anton pointed outside, and then turned to Lisa who raised her hand to stop him and said "Dear, I want to start unpacking. You all go and talk outside."

The men walked out and sat on the wooden chairs. Anton looked at the young men and said, "I've been impressed by your parents' decision to name you Oleg and Igor so that you would read history books and learn about the heritage of your names."

The brothers fidgeted in their chairs and stole a look at each other as Anton went on, "We had a son who was kidnapped when he was two years old, and we never heard from the kidnappers ..." he paused, as the brothers gasped.

"How terrible for you! I'm so sorry!" Oleg said, and Igor shook his head, "Horrible."

Anton looked down at his clasped hands. "It was a flourishing business twenty years ago for the *hunhuzi* and we are assuming that our boy was sold to a childless family." Anton pulled a handkerchief out of his pocket and dabbed at his eyes. "In memory of our son, my wife and I want to open a bank account in both of your names, so that you can go to Harbin to study at the institute and get a degree in history and engineering. You'll have all expenses paid while you study there, including housing. You will also be able to hire help for your parents in your absence."

"We can't leave our parents," Oleg said, and Igor nodded. "They need us. Father gets short of breath at the slightest effort, and Mother complains of pain in her legs. She stays mostly in the kitchen cooking, but there is much labor to do in the yard. Our cow needs to be milked and fed daily, the chicken coop needs to be cleaned, our produce to be distributed, and lots of other things."

Both young men sat with their mouths open, and then looked at each other with a searching look. Oleg spoke first. "As for your offer, one should go crazy happy from such manna from heaven. Igor and I don't deserve it. We love our work and our animals, and even call our cow Marfusha. We love our land and belong to it. As for our names, we read a lot about them and know that Princes Oleg and Igor were our early rulers in 900's and have been honored as such since then. We are proud to carry their names."

"We sure do, "Igor added when Oleg glanced at him, then went on, "We belong here, with our parents on this land, and so we shall be bringing brides into our home and will be expanding our house. So, please don't judge us being ungrateful. We are both overwhelmed by your generosity!"

Anton studied the brothers for a few moments, then said, "I understand your feelings. Well, there's another way we can help you. I will open an account in our bank in your names to draw the money as you need for payments on your property improvements."

"Your kindness is beyond words," Igor interrupted moving forward in his chair. "The first thing we need is to replace the rental cart and horse by buying our own. This rental expense cuts deeply into our income."

"Good. Then it is settled. And now how about some of that wonderful yeast *krendel* of your mother's?" Anton said with a smile and rose to get Lisa. She met him at the door to the kitchen with a smile and whispered to him, "I heard everything. I think it is wonderful."

After enjoying the cake, they went to their rooms where she hugged her husband without words. Anton kissed her. "I fretted a long time thinking what charity to invest in with all the surplus income we are accumulating, and now we have this wonderful family to care for."

"There's a lot to learn from these young men," Lisa said with a nod. "They taught us a valuable lesson by their honesty and no apology. Our life is not always the happiest, and we need these folks. We are lucky to have found them. Let's make a tour of all their property and see for ourselves what they urgently need besides buying the horse and buggy. And one more thing, let's keep this charity to ourselves for many reasons, one of which had been my father's warning not to let my left hand know what my right hand was doing.

They returned from their vacation glowing with happiness at what they had achieved and proceeded to set up a bank account for the Shubov brothers.

⌒

Months later, Lisa sat at her favorite bay window, watching the show of snowflakes lazily descending to earth and spreading their dazzling blanket over the cobblestones. Life settled into a gentle pace, keeping Lisa in contact with the Shubov family and all that they had achieved with the available funds. The parents, Ivan and Anna couldn't thank Anton and Lisa enough in their letters.

The friendship with the Jones' solidified between the two couples, and they exchanged visits frequently, enjoying each other's company. Nancy blossomed into a stunning beauty, her blue eyes rimmed with dark lashes and accentuated by golden hair that she had cut and styled into a short hairdo.

One day Jane confided in Lisa over the phone, that of all the young men who courted Nancy, both Russian and American, the most frequent date was a young Russian man who was hired recently by the consulate, and escorted Nancy to most of the receptions.

"What does David say about this?" asked Lisa sitting down on the chair provided for longer telephone chatting.

"Oh, you know how men are. He waved his hand at me, dismissing it. That's why I am sharing this with you over the phone now, while our husbands are at work."

"Let's see if anything develops further. In the meantime, I wouldn't say anything to Nancy. Let nature take its course."

"I really want you to meet him and tell me what you think. Why don't you and Anton drop by this afternoon for a drink? He is picking Nancy up to go to a movie, and you'll be able to tell me what you think."

"Alright, we'll drop by for a short while."

Lisa hung up the receiver with a smile and a shake of the head.

                                   ↬

When they arrived at the Jones' apartment, Lisa heard Jane say, "Nancy, wait a few minutes, the Platonovs have just arrived."

Lisa and Anton gave their coats to the maid and walked into the parlor. After Jane and David greeted them, and they sat down, David poured wine from a decanter on the coffee table and gave the glasses to them. He then turned toward Nancy's escort and led him toward Lisa and Anton, saying, "I want you to meet Nancy's new friend, Serezha Nikitin."

A jolt shook Lisa and she dropped her glass of wine over the carpet. "Oh. I'm so sorry, it slipped out of my hand!"

Jane quickly called the maid to mop up the wine, and then turned to Lisa. "It's white wine, Lisa, and the glass didn't break. No damage done." Then leaning over Lisa, she whispered, "Would you like a few drops of valerian?"

Lisa shook her head and frantically searched her shaken mind for a way to ask if the young man was adopted but couldn't find a way to do so without surprising everyone in the room. While she was arguing within herself as to the least suspicious way to voice her question, she overheard Serezha Nikitin laugh and say to Anton, "The joke in our family is that many friends say that my brother and I look alike, when in reality one of us is adopted, and my parents are secretive and reluctant to talk about it even with us, and even won't tell us which one of us is adopted. They keep telling us we are equal in their love for us, and that's that! So, we have long accepted it and think it's a good decision on the part of our parents."

But Lisa knew. It had to be Serezha. It had to be! The hazel eyes were looking at her now with a slight questioning look.

Lisa quickly turned towards Anton and knew she had to control herself and change the conversation to another topic. The revelation was too much for her. Realizing that she had found her son and yet could do nothing about it except be aware that he was well and living with a happy family, was torture. She couldn't catch her breath, and there were tears gathering behind her eyes, threatening to spill over. She tried to compose herself but knew she was on the verge of breaking down.

"I feel a little dizzy," she said, turning to Anton. "I think you better take me home." Lisa forced the words out, rising from the chair and leaning on Anton's arm. David brought Lisa's coat and helped her with it while Anton put on his own.

"Would you like me to call the doctor before you leave?" David asked, and when Anton shook his head, Jane came up and hugged Lisa. "I'll call you tomorrow," she said quietly.

Lisa and Anton said a quick good-bye and left. She wanted to talk about this further once they were alone, but there were constant interruptions the rest of the day, and at night she didn't want to get into such an emotional discussion before going to bed.

How could parents be so cruel, she thought, as to name that young man Serezha, to give him a brother, and not tell them which one is adopted? She thrashed in bed until the medicine she took worked its magic and helped her to fall into a restless sleep.

The next morning Jane called. "I'm so sorry dearest Lisa. Serezha is such a popular name, it just didn't occur to me to wonder … oh, how stupid of me, please forgive me! David never said anything about it either, so please think of it as a coincidence!"

"Please don't worry about it, Jane, it's just my active imagination, I guess, always overactive. He is a nice-looking young man, and I am sorry I reacted as I did. Let's just forget about it." They chatted a little more and then Lisa said, "Good-bye, see you soon" as she hung up.

That evening after supper, Lisa found time to talk to Anton as they sat in the parlor. "Anton, dearest, I can't dismiss this Serezha as my imagination. Not only the name, but an adoption, and the parents keeping it secret. There has to be a way to find out!"

"Nothing but pain would result for all of us. Please bury such a possibility and let the young people's courtship continue." *As long as their courtship does not progress any further* Lisa finished his sentence in her mind.

"Why don't we play chess until time to retire?" Anton said rising from his chair and offering Lisa his hand.

Lisa looked at the chess pieces waiting to be played on the other side of the room and rose to join her husband in their favorite game. Hours melted away and before she realized, it was time to retire.

⌒

A few weeks later, Jane invited them for supper. But Anton came home from his office earlier in a preoccupied mood and after Lisa told him of the Jones invitation, she asked him what was wrong. He waved her away with a curt retort, "Later Lisa, after we come home from the Jones'."

When Lisa and Anton arrived, at the Jones' Nancy and Serezha greeted them at the door. This time Lisa anticipated seeing the young couple together and braced herself for a tense visit. After they settled in the parlor over a glass of wine, Lisa could not resist asking Serezha if his brother was a hermit and didn't like company. She was afraid to look at Anton, because she knew he would be angry with her.

"As a matter of fact," said Serezha with a quick laugh, "Alexei, or Alesha as we call him, is a bookworm and prefers to bury himself in books."

Lisa persisted. "Are we never going to meet him then?"

Serezha chuckled. "I'll try to convince him that a gracious lady who is a dear friend of Nancy's family wants to meet him. We'll see what happens!"

Lisa smiled and only then looked at Anton with a gratified nod. Anton seemed distracted by his own thoughts and gave a slight shake of his head.

"Well, you may be more successful than we were!" Jane said.

The conversation moved toward the news of the day. The Russian newspaper, censored by the Japanese, had told them that morning in elaborate terms, of successful Japanese spread of control over Chinese land, and now their discussion was heavy with pessimism.

"There is really nothing we can do except lie low, and mind our own business," Anton said, and everyone agreed.

After a light meal, they all returned to the parlor for a glass of liqueur, but the atmosphere was depressing in the room, and when they finished their drinks, Anton and Lisa said good-bye to the Jones' and Serezha and left for home.

An uncomfortable silence hung in the air between them until they settled in their parlor and Anton dismissed the servants for the night. He then turned to Lisa, took her hands in his and cleared his throat, but before he could say a word, she pulled her hands out of his, and covering her face with both hands, turned toward the fireplace with a stifled cry, "I can't stand it!" Then turning toward Anton who started to pace the floor, she cried again, "I can't stand it!" with both arms stretched in a pleading gesture. "The whole time at the Jones' I wanted to look at him and say, "Serezha, you are my son. *My* son!"

Anton stopped abruptly and looked at Lisa. "He is *my* son as well, remember?"

An icy shiver rippled down Lisa's back. *My God, what is the matter with me? I nearly betrayed my deepest secret! I nearly caused a rupture in my life!*

A watershed of tears overwhelmed her, as she realized just how close she came to ruining her life and breaking Anton's heart.

Anton raised his weeping wife from her stooped position and hugged her. "We have each other, *golubka*. I too was wondering when I first saw Serezha Nikitin, but dismissed it as coincidence."

Now, leading Lisa to the loveseat, he sat her down and himself beside her. Dispensing with his usual endearing terms for his wife, he said, "My dear, it is time for us to stop speculating about the future and make plans for it." Anton's voice and demeanor were somber, and Lisa tensed.

"Your thoughts are still on Serezha," Anton said after lighting a cigarette. "What I will tell you has nothing to do with the Jones' family. It's about the Japanese authorities. A high-ranking Japanese officer approached me two days ago while I was taking a break from the office. I was a few paces from the gate entrance when he ordered me to show him my identification papers in a brusque tone of voice and loudly enough for all passers-by to hear. At the same time, he was moving me away from the gate to a more secluded spot. Once there, he switched from a sharp Japanese to a quiet and flawless Russian. He proceeded to give me detailed instructions for tomorrow when he intends to come to our house after dark, to inform us or maybe to prepare us for something the authorities are planning that will affect us."

Lisa covered her mouth with her hand and frowned as she listened to Anton with increasing alarm. Just as she tried to say to Anton how frightening that was, he raised his hand and shook his head.

"No questions, Lisa. I have no energy to talk tonight. I told you all I know. His directions were detailed, and I wrote them down, so tomorrow morning I will take a day off from the office and show them to you, so that we can discuss them with our minds clear."

Lisa knew when not to insist and, having kissed Anton on his forehead, left the room. Once upstairs, she reclined on her chaise lounge and tried to relax with a book of Pushkin verses before going to bed, but she knew in a few minutes that it wasn't going to work. She got up and paced the floor trying to think of some positive reason for the Japanese officer to be coming to see them after dark. Obviously, he was one of the more humane Japanese officers who wanted to warn and prepare them for whatever it was that he would tell them.

Lisa went to bed and turned the light out. The vigil light below the St. Nicholas icon hanging high in the right corner of the room, flickered soothingly and Lisa drifted into a light slumber with the thought that the Japanese officer was coming to help them.

Chapter 12

Lisa woke up in a daze, feeling disoriented for a few moments until the present situation hit her, and she rang for Agasha to help her get dressed. When she came down for breakfast, Anton was waiting for her. After breakfast, he led her to his den and closed the door.

It was Anton's private domain and Lisa rarely entered it except to check that the maid had left it in order after dusting. The room was furnished in Victorian style with leather upholstered chairs and couch. Along the walls were bookshelves filled with volumes on business, both legal and technical, on one side of the wall, and classics on the other. The light was dim in the room, giving it a solemn atmosphere. Lisa sat down in an armchair, opposite Anton who sat down at his desk and looked at her with a frown.

"I really don't know how to judge officer Shimura's visit, *golubka*," he said with a shake of his head. "With such elaborate secrecy, he obviously wants to protect himself from his superiors knowing of it. Anyway, here are his detailed instructions for tonight. He intends to arrive on foot at around eleven o'clock at night, and we should turn the lights out throughout the house. First, we should pretend that we are preparing to retire by turning the dining light out before the parlor, then one room after another, before going upstairs. After a while, we must turn the whole house into total darkness, as if we have gone to bed for the night. Then we should return downstairs and wait for him in our entry hall near the front door because he isn't going to ring the bell but knock on the door, avoiding awakening any servants. We are to sit in the entrance hall by the candlelight until he arrives and then listen to what he has to tell us.

Needless to say, you must behave yourself in a natural way throughout today. If anxiety overwhelms you, occupy yourself with your favorite poetry. It's best for me to return to the brewery with the excuse that I was delayed by some domestic problem."

"I understand," Lisa said in a shaky voice, "and I will tackle my overdue correspondence that I've neglected. If my nerves begin to show, I can always close my door."

Anton came around the desk to kiss her goodbye. Lisa quickly rose to hug him, and wrapping her hands around his neck, whispered, "We'll do exactly what the officer told you, darling. Let's keep a positive thought that nothing bad will come of it."

❦

The day dragged for Lisa while sorting her correspondence, hardly able to decide which invitation to accept and which to decline, while pushing aside the business envelopes for Anton to take care of later.

As the dining time approached, and Anton came home a few minutes after two, Lisa greeted him with an unusual strong embrace and the whisper of "My love, I'm so glad to see you," making sure the server didn't hear her. She hardly ate her meal, even though the soup was her favorite cucumber blend. Anton had to go back to the office and she was left once again to her own devices. Back in her room, she opened Lermontov's book of poetry but couldn't concentrate even on her favorite poem about the battle of *Borodino*. So she brought out her basket with a half-finished angora shawl and started to knit trying to fill the hours.

The increasing drops of rain tapped outside as twilight was settling over Harbin when Anton returned. Dark circles were clearly visible under his eyes and his slow movements spoke of fatigue. They ate a light supper, and then settled in the parlor. Anton picked up a few neglected magazines to look through, but for Lisa, reading was out of the question, so she called Agasha back and asked her to bring down her knitting from the bedroom, and then busied herself with the knitting pattern again.

Her heart refused to establish the slow rhythm she was used to and continued to jump erratically at the slightest noise. At long last, the clock showed ten, the usual time they prepared to retire for the night. Following the instructions to the letter, Lisa and Anton turned the lights out downstairs, one by one. Then upstairs, they were not to turn the lights out right away but wait several minutes to give the impression that they were preparing themselves for bed.

The ordeal was physically simple but nerve-wracking emotionally until they were ready to come downstairs again. Once in the kitchen, Anton picked up a kerosene lamp, instead of a candle, turned the flicker down to a minimum, and they sat down on folding chairs in the dark entry hall to wait.

"I forgot, what's his name?" Lisa whispered.

"Col. Shimura," Anton replied. "You better not greet him by name and don't speak unless spoken to."

When the front door knock sounded, Anton opened the door and let the uniformed officer in. Lisa bowed slightly and silently offered him an empty chair. He nodded and taking his cap off, sat down.

"Where did you get this antiquity?" He asked gruffly, pointing at the kerosene lamp.

"We have a small *dacha* on the other side of Sungari, and we use it when we stay there for a few days." Anton cleared his throat and added, "You speak Russian very well."

Shimura shifted in his chair and said, "I went to school in Vladivostok. It helps here in Harbin. I don't approve of my superiors' methods of persuasion on people who are on our list to be questioned. As you can see from my presence here tonight, I'm not one of the Japanese who is notorious for their cruelty. At our recent meeting, several names of Russians have come up to contact in the near future and yours is one of them." Col. Shimura gave Lisa a quick glance and then continued, "That is why I am here, to warn and prepare you for what they want from you. Your brewery has prospered and aroused our interest. When your turn comes up to contact you, they will offer to buy it for what they say will be an excellent price, and they will give you several weeks to contact all your shareholders and prepare the sale formalities."

"And if I refuse to sell?"

"What they will offer you will be minimal, as was with other enterprises, but if you refuse…." Shimura shook his head, frowned, and then said, "The alternative would be worse."

Lisa shuddered, remembering various rumors they had heard. She glanced at Anton and saw that his face had blanched as he cleared his throat and asked, "How much time do we have before they act on my brewery?"

"Your name is down the long list, and that is why I came to see you now. Think carefully of what alternative you may have, if any, and be prepared for them."

Col. Shimura rose, put his cap on, and with a curt nod left the house.

Lisa wanted to run after him with questions, but Anton blocked her way and said, "He told us all he could, and more questions would only annoy him, to our detriment. Let's try to digest all he told us tomorrow. He was good to give us weeks to form a plan and in the meantime I have something in mind to talk to you about."

He took Lisa's hand in a firm grasp and led her upstairs. In her bedroom, he released her hand. "Please take valerian drops and think of good thoughts. I have an idea about the brewery and I will tell you about it tomorrow. It's too long to explain to you now, when it's so late and we need our clear heads to discuss it. Try to sleep."

With that, Anton kissed her and left for his bedroom.

Chapter 13

The next morning Anton told her at breakfast that they would talk that night as he needed to be at the brewery on time that day. He kissed her on the forehead and left.

Lisa didn't know how to occupy herself for the rest of the day without dwelling on the problem of successful escape. On such short notice, where could they possibly find a hiding place without being found by the Japanese, who seemed to be everywhere, in towns, in villages, in various resorts. And what did Anton have up his sleeve to be so sure of himself? Whatever he had, it was complicated. He came home at 2 o'clock but kept her agonizing until the evening. Neither poetry nor knitting worked to help move the crawling hours faster.

At last, the grandfather's clock downstairs chimed twice, and Lisa hurried down to wait for Anton. When he came in however, he seemed preoccupied with his thoughts and answered Lisa with a monotone of yes's and no's, so she gave up on any dialogue and they finished their meal in silence.

"I'm sorry, dear, but I shall explain everything to you tonight. You'll understand then." Anton sealed his short statement with a kiss, then picked up his leather briefcase and with the words "See you tonight" thrown over his shoulder, left the house.

Lisa didn't say a word, so unused she was to that distant husband she had never seen before. She did not take offense to his change of attitude, for she instinctively realized that Anton was seriously preoccupied with major decisions in their lives and all that was going to be discussed with her that night. She made herself turn to domestic chores, gave instructions to the servants for the rest of the next few hours, and finally was able to settle down in the parlor to wait for Anton with a glass of wine. It felt good to divert her attention away from the dim future, which she could not control anyway. This time, the book she wanted to read was Anna Karenina. She was taken by the heroine's audacity to leave her husband and ruin her reputation for the sake of illicit love. Lisa was so engrossed in the story that she was startled when she heard the clock chime seven. Anton should be coming home any minute.

She closed the book and headed toward the entry hall as Anton was coming in. His face was still somber, and the usual greeting smile was hidden behind his pressed lips. Almost immediately he called Agasha to bring them their supper. A tureen of borscht accompanied by a platter of piroshky wafted a familiar, mouth-watering aroma, that both of them always enjoyed. This time, however, Anton showed no appreciation for their favorite meal. They ate in silence and Lisa consumed her meal quickly, watching her husband as he finished his supper without taking a second helping, which had been his usual habit.

When he called for Agasha, he told her to clear the dishes and not to bother with dessert. "Tell everyone that you are all finished with the day's work. We shall retire upstairs." He nodded briefly and rose to help Lisa away from the table. With each silent gesture, dark clouds of storm darkened around him, and Lisa followed upstairs without saying a word. Once in her bedroom, they sat down in their favorite chairs and Lisa clasped her hands tightly, well aware that whatever her husband told her was not going to be to her liking.

Anton pulled his armchair closer to Lisa's, took her hand and kissed it. "*Golubka,*" he said, "we do have a solution for escaping the Japanese purchase proposal if we act immediately. You see, dearest, some time ago, I received a letter from the CEO of a brewery in Northern California in America, offering to merge my brewery with his at a generous price. With it, a large house to rent until we get settled, orient ourselves, and decide on a house to buy. It sounded too good to be true. I wondered how he heard of me, and there, at the end of the letter he mentioned that he had tasted a bottle of an imported beer that he liked, and it happened to be mine."

"I toyed with the idea of going to California to see what it's like over there, but since we learned that the Japanese have their eye on my brewery, the American offer took on a different meaning. I have already signed the agreement and predated it and opened an account at the Bank of America in San Francisco, where we already have the down payment deposited. So, if the officials come up with their offer, I will be able to show them that they were late, and my brewery is already in the American's possession." Anton lit a cigarette and took a deep drag. "It would be even better if the full payment confirmation arrives before we hear from the Japanese."

Lisa listened with wide open eyes, and when he finished, she said, "I can't believe that you are ready to abandon our search for Serezha just when we are so close to identifying him! You are ready to pack up and leave everything behind, our mini-Russia, and everything we know and love here! You didn't even mention our son during your whole speech. How could you?"

Anton rose abruptly and looked down on her. "I'm tired of your single-minded attitude. I have grieved for our son for a very long time. Now, I am comforted to know that he has loving parents."

He lit a cigarette, then went on, "That's why I dealt with the Americans and the Bank of America before telling you. Think of what you're doing! Now you want to cause an upheaval in the young man's life because of your selfish obsession. Think of what we are facing if we stay here and do nothing."

Lisa shrank in her armchair and stared at her husband. A cold tremor of fear with all of its threats poured over her. She lowered her head and whispered, "I'm sorry. Oh my God, so much all at once. I'm so scared, Antosha! What must we do first? How much time do we have?"

The use of his pet name cooled Anton's anger. He knelt before her chair and said, "Mr. Tomason, the CEO, said in his letter he recognizes how much work is involved for us, and we can have two months to liquidate everything. He also said that I can offer my shareholders, knowledgeable in their own way of making beer, an opportunity to join me if they wish to resettle in California. As to how we should begin, we should keep this plan secret from as many people as possible until the Japanese approach me with their offer. I hope that by then the full payment for the merger will be deposited in our account at the Bank of America. The Japanese' hands will be tied when they realize that my brewery is lost to them."

Lisa could tell how difficult it was for him to deal with these monumental decisions. She hugged him and whispered, "I am here for you, darling, tell me where and how to begin. We have two months, you said, so at least we won't flee like refugees! Tell me first, who can know about our leaving," Lisa's voice broke, she coughed and recovered, "I'm sorry that it gets me once in a while, but I simply cannot chase my fighting thoughts away... Serezha... Harbin... Jones'... all other friends, our loyal servants... and the Shubovs in Handaohedzi... I must not dwell on all of this and yet the thoughts drum their beat without order in my brain… so please tell me whom may I tell first?" Lisa looked up into Anton's stressed face with a pleading look.

Anton stroked her hair, "*golubka,* we have no alternative but trust our servants. Loyal as they are, it's only human to be tempted to share such news with close relatives or friends, so you must frighten them by disclosing Col. Shimura's warning. Not only that, but you have to impress upon them how to be silent by reminding them of what happened to the shareholders of large businesses who were forced to sell as well."

Everything that happened so far had been a forewarning of the future, and Lisa tossed in her bed all night, sleeping fitfully, nightmares of Shimura making fun of her in front of others telling her she and Anton were now their prisoners.

She woke up bathed in sweat, heart pounding after that nightmare, a reminder to get active immediately. As Anton said, the first people to include into their painful odyssey were the servants.

When Agasha came in, Lisa could tell by the look on her face that their loyal maid had noticed her Barinya was upset, and stood silently, waiting for orders.

"We are in deep trouble, Agasha," Lisa said, and proceeded to tell her about the warning they had received about the officials planning to buy their brewery.

Agasha moaned, "Oh no, Barinya, how can they do that?"

"They can and they will. That is why Baryn and I wanted to tell you about this, to warn you to be silent and not to divulge any of this to anyone. Just remember what happened to the shareholders of large businesses when they refused to sell."

When Lisa told her about their imminent departure for America, Agasha burst into tears. "What am I going to do,

Barinya, without you? You have been my family for so long, I'll be lost without you!" "We'll find a new family to take you in, don't worry. Tell the rest of our staff what I told you and how vital it is for us to keep all this secret until Barin receives his full payment for the brewery.

Then we shall be relatively safe from the officials' pressure."

Agasha sniffed, wiped her eyes with the edge of her apron. "And … and Serezha?"

Lisa burst into tears, controlled herself with difficulty, and then said, "This is not going to change, Agasha … let's start sorting my clothes … what to take and what to leave behind for the needy."

The two women buried themselves in sorting Lisa's clothing, but before long it became daunting and Agasha straightened her back and faced Lisa with a shaking head. "I'm sorry. Barinya, it will take the two of us much longer than we thought. We need Dasha to sort the good from the used underwear and for you to decide which ones to reject and which ones to launder and to take along. The trouble is you can't take all your clothes. Also, you have to tell me what to do with your rejects."

Lisa straightened up too, sat hard on her bed, and said, "You are right. Go down to the kitchen and meet me with everyone in the parlor."

⤳

This time, it was Agasha who relayed all the information to the rest of the servants. Having given authority to her maid, Lisa felt that the rest of the servants would accept the importance of keeping it all secret since Agasha had accepted it, and all the future news would be filtered to them through her. Dasha sniffled and wiped her eyes with the back of her hand. The Chinese cook, having recently converted to Christianity, crossed himself, bowed to Lisa, and said, "We hear what the Japanese can do to people. You don't worry, Barinya, we're all loyal to you and Barin and none of us will betray you!"

Lisa nodded, thanked them all and sent the cook back to the kitchen but kept Dasha and Agasha to continue sorting the clothes. The work moved much faster and they were close to finishing.

For a few days the loyal servants worked in various parts of the house and evolved into a family unit without complaint or intrusion into the privacy of their master's life. Anton and Lisa felt supported by the affection of all their servants, and no longer felt isolated from the rest of the world. The day came, however, when all the work that needed to be done prior to the final packing was finished. Lisa could only hope that the Americans had sensed the urgency and would expedite the final payment for the merger. Anton had already prepared a letter of thanks. It was sealed and stamped, and all it needed was to be mailed without losing a single day.

Chapter 14

September sunshine caressed the group in Anton's house, where the servants went about their business as if nothing had happened. Dasha reported that the owner of the bakery, a hefty woman in her forties, had pinpointed her eyes on her, and pressed for an answer of why her friend looked so drawn in her face. Dasha shook her head, "I told her that I had a headache and couldn't fall asleep for a long time. I hope she accepted that."

"Don't worry," Lisa said, "as long as we keep quiet, no harm done. Our work inside the house is quiet and there is nothing for us to do until we get the letter that we are waiting for. Every day when Barin comes home for dinner, I keep hoping he will bring the letter from America with him. Let's hope today will be a lucky day!" She smiled and sent Dasha back to the kitchen, after which Lisa settled in the parlor with the last section of Anna Karenina, but the printed words swam before her eyes and made no sense. She closed the novel, reclined in her loveseat and closed her eyes.

Loyal servants, Lisa thought, where would they work after we leave Harbin? And what about Serezha? Oh, God, Anton was right, they must not disrupt their son's established life with the only parents he remembered, especially when they were about to leave him anyway. As soon as the letter from America arrived, they would go to the Jones' and share the news with them. They would be delighted to hear that we'd be living in their country.

She rose to go upstairs, but at the same time the front door flew open, and Anton burst forward with a smile, holding a foreign looking envelope high in his hand. Grabbing Lisa's hand, they went to the den and closed the door behind them. "The payment is in the Bank of America, and the proof is here!" Anton pulled the letter out of the envelope and showed it to Lisa, after which he replaced it and put it away in the small safe that he kept near his desk.

"On sober thought," Anton said turning toward Lisa, "we mustn't broadcast our imminent departure and attract Japanese attention to ourselves. They will approach me soon enough and I must act surprised and reveal that my brewery has been already sold."

"But Anton, darling, we must tell our news to the Jones' for two reasons. They'll be hurt if we don't share it with them right away, and second, Jane will be of tremendous help in telling me about American customs and what to expect when we get to San Francisco."

Anton looked at Lisa with an unfocused look and sighed. "Of course, you're right darling, and we must both go to see them. While you visit with Jane, I can talk to David and tell him about my merger with the American brewery."

The Jones' were shocked and pleased to hear the news and urged Anton and Lisa to reveal the details of how everything happened. After they did, David asked Anton, "Have you told the Japanese authorities about the merger yet?"

"Not yet but will do in a day or so."

David shook his head vigorously, "NO! You must do it at once, Anton, before they come to you with their own offer for buying. I was present during several discussions between our

Consul and the Japanese officials and witnessed how far they went to great lengths to avoid losing face. At all costs, you must prevent them from coming to you with a purchase offer and find the brewery already merged with Americans, and in the process of being closed. Such a scene would surely antagonize them and provoke revenge."

Lisa and Jane stopped chatting and listened intently to the men.

David spoke with such vehemence that Anton nodded and said, "My God! With all the excitement of the last few days, this trait of their character slipped my mind." He paused to light a cigarette, and then shook his head, "How could I forget it!"

"Well, don't delay now, go at once!"

Anton extinguished his cigarette in a little tray, and after patting David's shoulder, kissed Jane's hand good-bye. Lisa tried to hug her friend, when Jane stopped them with a smile. "Wait a minute. We too have something to share with you that no one knows as yet. Please sit down both of you. It won't take but a few minutes."

Surprised by Jane's words and David's sudden smile, Anton and Lisa paused and sat down.

"I was going to wait until we had more details before telling you," David said, but I see how eager Jane is to share the news with you, so here it is. We decided to resign my position at the consulate here and return to the States permanently. My mother has a large home in Pasadena and is delighted to have us stay with her until I am assigned to another post."

Anton asked, "What made you decide to leave your good position here?"

"It's not the job I have, but the general political situation in China that has been worrying us. We were blinded by how easily Harbin fell to them after a small exchange of gunfire in the Modyagow section. But now the violence of Japanese occupation reaches all of us through underground news. When we heard of the massacre in Nanking, however, that was the last straw. We decided to go home while we can. Nancy's birthday is coming up and a party has been planned, so after that is over, we shall be leaving soon after. We insist that you visit us in Pasadena."

"We won't take no for an answer," added Jane, "You'll be tired after the long ocean crossing, and will need to get your energy back before starting a new life."

Stunned and pleased by the Jones' news, Anton shook his head on the way home. "How could I have forgotten that important facet of the Japanese character! I'll drop you off at home, pick up the proof of the merger, and do the unpleasant job."

At home, he rushed to their safe, pulled out the necessary paperwork, and left for the Japanese headquarters.

Lisa smiled at the thoughts that invaded her mind. David, whom she had wanted to avoid for many years only to discover that he was just as anxious to conceal their affair as she had been for many years. Now, she spent the empty hours moving aimlessly from room to room, cataloging in her mind the bric-a-brac that were yet to be packed, leaving the furniture to be shipped by professionals.

In spite of acute longing to contact her many friends, Lisa kept a rigid hold on such temptation, and knew she had to wait for Anton's return with the result from his interview with Japanese officials.

When Anton returned, he was smiling. "I outwitted the SOB's. I had a hunch that they would want to take my American papers under the pretext of checking them and I feared that I would never see them again. So, when the letter arrived, the first thing I did was make copies of the paperwork.

The duplicates I showed the official disappeared in his desk drawer, and as I showed my immediate concern about them, the stern Japanese official barked that they would keep them a few days and I was to come back for them when he called"

Anton lit a cigarette and added, "What a narrow escape that was, darling. I can't tell you how relieved I am to have made copies!"

Lisa put her arms around Anton's neck and kissed him. "*Antosha*, I'm so happy things are working out. In the meantime, what can we do about the Shubovs? I mean I am wondering about the money we have for them in the local bank. Are we going to be able to deposit the funds from America?"

"David assured me that the Japanese authorities are always courteous to the Consul, so there seems to be no problem, when the money will be coming from America. If things change, the Shubovs are well off already and they can get along without our help. In the meantime, we'll keep depositing funds to them for their future needs. We must spend our last summer with them and tell them goodbye. It will be a wrenching one, but we must brace ourselves to make our parting as smooth as we can."

They left shortly before the sandstorm enshrouded Harbin to spend the summer with the Shubovs. On the train Lisa was lulled by the rhythmic knocking of the wheels, trying to immerse herself in the beauty of the stately evergreen forest that the train cut through. Anton was deep in his own thoughts until they reached their beloved Handaohedzi.

Lisa's heart squeezed painfully at the thought of what news they were bringing but kept smiling all the way from the train station to the Shubov's house, preceded by a tempting fragrance of borscht and *krendel*, followed by another round of hugs from Ivan and Anna.

"You came a couple of weeks earlier than usual. Are you bringing us some special news?" asked Ivan, looking from Anton to Lisa and back.

"Yes, we have a lot to tell you, but let's finish this delicious meal first," Anton replied in a quiet voice, and concentrated on eating the hot borscht. Lisa ate silently beside him.

Once they finished eating, there was no avoiding the inevitable. Anton took Lisa's hand and cleared his throat. "I have been contacted by a brewery in America offering to merge with them in California at impossible to refuse conditions. Since the Japanese are beginning to take over large enterprises, I signed the contract. We have two months to complete our transaction and move to America. We came to tell you all this and assure you that your deposits will continue, but even if they stop due to political changes, I am sure you will have enough funds for a long time. I can't begin to tell you how sad we are to say goodbye, but we'll keep in contact with you as long as our correspondence continues to go through."

The Shubovs were quiet for a few moments, and then Oleg spoke, "We are of course shocked and sad to see you leave us. Financially, you are right, we are in good shape, thanks to your generosity. Even if deposits stop, you have already made it possible for us to be well situated and we can manage by our own efforts."

The brothers hugged Anton and Lisa, while Anna and Ivan wiped their eyes. "The Lord be with you on your journey," Ivan said making a sign of the cross. "We hope you will write to us."

"We shall look forward to getting your first letter," Anna continued, and rose to clear the dishes. The two brothers rose also, and Oleg said, "Would you like to see some of the things that we were able to do because of your help?"

Lisa and Anton followed the brothers to the yard. Lisa opened her eyes wide in surprise. "This is wonderful what you've accomplished here."

"Incredible!" seconded Anton shaking his head.

The dilapidated chicken coop was replaced with a new one, lacquered to protect it from the elements, and the new cowshed amply covered their cow and the person who would milk her. Anton made numerous admiring comments and Lisa echoed him. After the tour was completed, they resumed their routine for the rest of the summer, and when the time came to return to Harbin, they bid the Shubovs a reluctant goodbye, promising to write as soon as they could.

Immersed in their own sadness, they didn't speak on the train until they reached Harbin. Agasha met them at the door with the news that Mistress Jones called several times, asking if Lisa was home yet. "She seemed excited but didn't say anything more except ask to be called back as soon as you got home."

"Did she sound worried?" Lisa asked.

"No, Barinya, on the contrary, she sounded happy."

Lisa smiled. Obviously, there was something pleasant that Jane wanted to share with her, and it would be wonderful to break away from her troubling thoughts.

The phone rang only twice before Jane answered it, and Lisa said, "Jane, dear, we just walked through the door when Agasha told me you called. What's all the excitement?"

"Oh, I'm so glad to hear your voice! Nancy's birthday is coming up and she waited too long to tell me that she wants to have a big party to celebrate her 20th with music and dancing. There's no time to print and distribute invitations, so I'm saddled to phone all our friends with the invitations! Can you imagine that light-headed child? I've been sitting at this phone until my finger has gotten sore from all the dialing. I just hope you have enough time to pick your gown or to assemble a new outfit. There are ten days yet left so I hope you and Anton will join us."

Lisa hung up the receiver with a broad smile. What a marvelous event that will be, she thought, exactly what they needed, a happy dinner dance to set aside all the tribulations and fears of the past several weeks. Her emotions could take just so much before her ailing heart would rebel and cause trouble, just what she didn't need at that time. She looked through her evening gowns, pulled out several dressy ones in pastel colors and selected a blue silk one, trimmed with lace. She had a pair of matching silk shoes and beaded purse. As she held the delicate fabric in her hands, her face glowed with a happy smile. Anton had gone to retrieve his American bank papers, and she was waiting to tell him about Jane's call.

She went downstairs and sat in the parlor to wait for her husband.

Chapter 15

Although Anton braced himself for the encounter with the Japanese official, it turned out worse than he expected. First, he waited for almost an hour to be seen, and when admitted to the officer's office, he faced an angry and different man from the one to whom he had given the copy of the American letter.

"What do you want?" barked the Japanese, glaring at Anton.

"I came to pick up my American letter."

"What letter?"

"The letter from the American Bank."

"No letter here. Go away!"

"I left it with the other officer who was here."

The Japanese officer jumped up, pushing his chair back so it fell on the floor, spread his arms apart and leaning the palms of his hands on his desk, yelled, "No letter! Out!"

Instead, Anton took a step forward and said as calmly as he could, "I repeat, that letter came from an American bank, and if you don't find it in your files or drawers, I'll telegraph the bank in San Francisco and tell them that you refused to return it."

The inflated balloon of fury was punctured, and a considerably subdued Japanese officer picked up his chair, sat down without looking at Anton and after looking through several drawers, pulled out a file and drew the letter out. He glanced at it and threw it across the desk toward Anton. "Get out! Don't come back!"

Anton didn't waste any time and left the office, closing the door firmly behind him. No use testing his luck by further aggravating the man with any dialogue he thought. The first drops of September rain cooled his face, and he smiled at the thought that the letter was in his hands even though it was only a copy.

When Anton entered the house, Lisa's one look at his beaming face was enough without wasting words.

"Agasha," called Anton, "go to the wine cellar and bring up a bottle of Veuve Cliquot for our supper tonight."

Lisa laughed and ran upstairs to change into a navy silk dressing gown and joined Anton, who had also changed into his maroon velvet smoking jacket.

The supper was happy and after they ate, they enjoyed a game of chess. As usual, Anton won, but Lisa had fun anyway.

⌇

The next day, the routine of packing continued with sober thoughts of what to take with them and what was to be shipped later. The servants were happy for the Platonovs, but heartbroken to lose them, in spite of other families Anton had found who were happy to have them.

The days flew by, filled with minutia of visiting close friends to say goodbye and writing notes to many acquaintances, until finally, Lisa told Anton that her job was done, and the only chores left were his. The day of Nancy's birthday came upon them. They stood before the mirror in Lisa's room admiring her golden ball gown, and Anton in his white tie and tails.

'We've come a long way. *Golubka*," Anton said with a smile. "Time to go. We don't want to be too late and make a grand entrance."

Riding with Anton in their car, Lisa speculated as to why Jane and David were throwing such a lavish ball for Nancy's birthday. After all, birthdays come every year, so why in particular this one? A vague disturbance crawled into her mind, but she forced herself to direct her thoughts on what Nancy would be wearing on her festive day.

As they approached the consulate, music sounded outside inviting guests to come in. Lisa threaded her arm through Anton's hurrying up the steps and moving her shoulders to the rhythm of a foxtrot.

Once inside, she was dazzled by the sight of women's elaborate ball gowns, men's white tie and tails outfits, and the changing rhythms of dance music.

As they entered into the festive hall, they were greeted at the head of the receiving line by the Consul and his wife and next to them stood the beaming David, Jane and Nancy.

"The Consul heard it was Nancy's special birthday and wanted to take over the celebration!" whispered Jane.

Lisa exchanged air kisses with Jane and stepped down to the dining hall to look for their assigned seats. In a few minutes all the guests were seated, and the Consul invited everyone to start eating. The meal was sumptuous and consumed by everyone with obvious relish. At the end of the meal, the Consul rose with a glass of champagne and congratulated Nancy on her twentieth birthday, wishing her many successful years ahead.

"And now," he said, "I pass the microphone to my loyal Secretary, David Jones, who has a personal announcement to make." With that he handed the microphone to David, who rose to accept it with a smile.

"Ladies and Gentlemen, I too wish Nancy a happy birthday. But in addition, it is with great pleasure that I announce my daughter's engagement to Sergei Nikitin, an engineer in our consulate. Please raise your glass to cheer the young couple with me and my wife."

Lisa's heart thumped painfully. *No! Not Serezha! Oh, Lord, my God! This is my Nemesis!* She dropped her glass of champagne as an impenetrable darkness descended upon her, wiping out all thought with a sudden tortuous pain in her chest that plunged her into unconsciousness.

⤚

Lisa was taken to the hospital. Semi-conscious most of the time, she thrashed around in her bed, fighting nightmares, mumbling words through tears, crying out "No," and "Don't!" until Dr. Semenov gave her a strong injection to calm her. He was the only one of course, who knew the cause of her agony and why the marriage had to be avoided. He was at an impasse himself, whether to break his Hippocratic oath or allow a genetic crime to take place.

Several hours later, Lisa opened her eyes and groggily looked at the doctor with slow recognition. Before she was able to say anything, the doctor put his finger against his lips to silence her and whispered, "Others will hear you. Wait until the nurses leave and then we shall talk."

The doctor closed the door. "The wedding is not to take place until all the paperwork is processed, due to Serezha's lack of citizenship, so we have time to decide on what course of action to take. The most important thing now is to get you stabilized with medication."

Lisa grabbed the edge of the doctor's jacket and whispered, "How can we stop the marriage without someone else knowing the truth?"

"Let me delve into all possibilities available to us, Lisa. I am sure there is something we'll be able to do. There is one thing in our favor, and that is the fact that Serezha and Nancy are half siblings, with only his father in common. Come to think of it, there are several royal families in Europe who are guilty of that genetic problem. Leave it to me to work it out and try to rest in the meantime."

Dr. Semenov left Lisa's room and once outside took a *droshky* to the Nikitin's residence. Relaxing in the comfortable carriage behind the bearded Russian driver urging on his obedient horse, the doctor was glad these men still kept their trade in spite of the availability of taxis

At the Nikitin's house, a maid opened the door and led him to a Victorian furnished parlor where Serezha's parents greeted him formally, trying to hide their surprise by the unannounced visit. Mrs. Nikitin was a short lady with chestnut hair and dark eyes, and her heavy-set husband towered above her.

Without any preamble, Dr. Semenov launched into a fabricated story of genetic research, and said he was fascinated by the glaring differences in the brothers' personalities. He explained that he had met Sergei and only heard about Alexei who stayed away from all receptions.

The parents laughed. "Small wonder," Mrs. Nikitin said, "the boys are not related at all because we adopted Alexei when he was two years old. To give him a new start in life we changed his original name of Sergei to Alexei, and named our own son Sergei, born shortly after we adopted Alexei. So, here is your genetic mystery unraveled."

In spite of his dignified demeanor, the doctor clapped his hands with the jubilant "Oh! I see!"

"I only wish," she continued, "you could have met Alexei before he left for his studies in Australia. He has always been a serious student with excellent grades. He plans to be here for Sergei's wedding, so perhaps you'll meet him there."

"I had always encouraged him to pursue his chosen profession," added Mr. Nikitin. "We are indeed very proud of him."

"Thank you for explaining all this to me. Now I have to hurry back to the clinic and attend to my patients." The doctor said goodbye and left in a hurry.

Instead of the clinic, however, he went directly to see Lisa.

⤳

When visitors were allowed, Jane went to see Lisa, raving about how happy Nancy and Serezha were. Those words sliced away a piece of Lisa's hard-earned recuperation, but she was able to give Jane a weak nod and a poor attempt at a smile.

"Due to our immediate departure for the States as soon as Serezha's visa comes through, we shall be going for Shanghai where we'll board a ship for San Francisco and from there on to Pasadena to my mother-in-law's home. We shall expect you to visit us first thing upon your arrival." It took a few minutes of idle chatter for Jane to realize that Lisa hadn't said a word all that time. Awkwardly, she changed the subject and rose to leave. "I must run my errands now, Lisa. You rest now, dear friend, and I must say goodbye." With a light kiss on Lisa's forehead, Jane left, and Lisa fell back on her pillows exhausted.

.No sooner than she was able to control herself and take the pills, Dr. Semenov came in and closed the door behind him. Pulling a chair close to her bed, he took her hand into his and said, "My dear one, all our worries are over," and with that proceeded to tell her of his visit to Serezha's home. "And now," he added in conclusion, "your recuperation should be rapid, and you should be able to leave for America as planned."

With tears of happiness cascading down her cheeks, Lisa could not speak and only squeezed his hand, and hugged the doctor with the other arm. After a few minutes, she smiled and said, "I can hardly wait to tell this to Anton! He'll be so happy!"

But the doctor shook his head and said, "No, no! You must see your son alone before you tell Anton about Alexei. What if he turns out to be blond? With both you and Anton being brown-eyed and dark haired, you will have to keep this a secret forever. Let's just hope he has your coloring." Dr. Semenov extricated himself from the embrace and after patting Lisa's hand, promised to see her the next day. Lisa's excitement vanished at the possibility of keeping the truth from Anton forever.

Chapter 16

Lisa's recovery seemed surprisingly fast to everyone except to Dr. Semenov, who discharged Lisa from the hospital a few days later with instructions to be cautious with her activities. The servants were elated to see their Barinya home and couldn't do enough for her. All her favorite food was carefully prepared. Lisa enjoyed all the attention.

One day, Jane called to invite them to Nancy and Serezha's civil service ceremony. "It's unexpected, but we want to leave China."

Lisa gasped in surprise, but Jane went on, "Nancy had her big birthday party, and now a civil marriage will have to suffice. Serezha's brother, Alexei, is coming to be the best man and witness, so there will be a small celebration for all of us while we are all together."

Lisa had trouble with her voice as it trembled with excitement at the prospect of finally meeting her son. "Of course we'll come, dear Jane. We look forward to it."

At the end of the phone call, Lisa's hand shook as she replaced the receiver on its base and went upstairs holding onto the railing to steady herself. Once in her room, she reclined in her chaise lounge and tried to find a way to control her emotions. Suddenly, her memory went into action and brought up a vision of herself at the age of seven, standing straight with tightly clenched fists in front of the nanny and listening to her scolding. It was a simple and full proof solution. Lisa got up and practiced squeezing her fists hard enough to stop the tremor. Relieved, she went to her boudoir where all her clothes were and started to look for an outfit that would be appropriate to wear to a civil marriage. After much indecision, she selected her silk two-piece suit in her favorite peach color with a matching pillbox hat and sat downstairs to wait for Anton to come home and tell him of Jane's phone call.

Anton's reaction was cautious. "Civil marriage is legal in America." he said, " I hope Serezha will want a church wedding as well after they get settled in Pasadena."

∽

On the day of the marriage ceremony, Lisa's tremor increased, and her fingernails dug deeper into her palms as she kept her fists clenched. They arrived at the consulate early and sat waiting for the wedding group to arrive. It wasn't long before the door opened and the Justice of the Peace stepped into the room followed by Nancy, wearing a white silk suit and a lace veil over her head. She was followed by Serezha in a white tuxedo, and next to him, was his brother Alexei, in a black tuxedo.

Lisa held her fists even tighter as she looked at Alexei. With an unexpected shock, she saw herself reflected in the young man's face. There was no doubt that she was looking at her beloved, lost child. Her image in Alexei's face made it undeniable. Lisa had to exert great effort and reluctance to look away from Alexei, hoping that no one would notice the resemblance. She looked around at the attending guests and settled her glance on an older couple sitting in the front row next to Jane and David. It took no effort to guess that these were Serezha's parents, the Nikitins.

They were surrounded by an aura of such happiness, that Lisa's heart was pierced with jealousy for not being the one who had brought up Alexei from a two-year old toddler to this handsome young man. Then she heard the words, "I now pronounce you man and wife, you may kiss the bride. The Nikitins went up to the new-lyweds and kissed and hugged them, followed by Jane and David. They were all conservatively dressed, the men in tailored suits, Jane in a beige colored suit and hat, and Mrs. Nikitin in a blue one.

Lisa and Anton lined up behind them and when their turn came, kissed Nancy, hugged Serezha, and shook hands with Alexei. Lisa's natural reaction was to hug Alexei, instead she said quietly, "We're so happy to meet you at last!"

Alexei smiled shyly and said, "I'm glad to meet you too. Sergei told me how kind you've been to David and Jane."

A luncheon followed in the dining room, but Alexei and the two pairs of parents, crowded the newlyweds so Lisa never got a chance to talk to Alexei, or "Alesha" as she already called him in her mind. After the luncheon, she was able to get near him and asked how long he'd be in Harbin.

Alexei said, "The newlyweds are going to spend three days in Imyanpo, so I already said goodbye to my parents and will be with Nancy's parents before leaving for Australia."

Lisa and Anton excused themselves and left the consulate to go home. All the way, Lisa thought of various ways to tell Anton why she didn't tell him about Alexei. She knew that no matter how she explained her silence until now, he would be angry and hurt. Once at home, Lisa took some Valerian drops to fortify herself for the task of telling him she knew that Alexei was their son. She called down to Anton and asked him to come up to her bedroom for greater privacy from the servants' listening ears.

Her husband's surprised and eager look made it even harder for her to speak, but finally, she said, "Darling, what I am about to tell you, is going to thrill you, but also hurt you. Please concentrate on the happy news!"

119

"Well, you certainly gave me a contrary introduction. I can't wait, what is it?"

"Alexei *is* our son! I already call him Alesha in my mind."

"How do you know?"

Lisa rubbed her hands nervously and proceeded to talk fast, telling him the whole story starting with Dr. Semenov's visit to the Nikitins' house and what they had told him about switching names. Anton rose from his chair and stood over her. "My God, how could you! Didn't you have any concern for me? You made me look like a fool, shaking his hand formally when that was my own son! You selfish… selfish woman… you only think of yourself! I pampered you all these years… never told you of my own pain about losing our son… and you're repaying me with this… this humiliation!"

"No, no, no, Antosha, please hear me out! He doesn't know about us yet. I asked to see him tomorrow while the newlyweds are gone, and we can tell him about us together. We'll have a wonderful reunion. Please, my dearest, forgive me for hurting you inadvertently. I meant well. Dr. Semenov warned me to wait and save you a bitter disappointment because Alesha might have turned out to be blond. That would have told me that Alexei is not our son. At least this way only I would have been disappointed.

Anton stared at Lisa for a few moments, and then sighed deeply. "Forgive me, I had such a shock. A left-handed surprise I'd call it, Lisa. What a good-looking young man he grew up to be. But how can you be sure that Alexei is really our son? Just because he has darker hair and eyes?"

Lisa smiled. "Wait till you look at him closely," she said. "I thought I was looking in a mirror, he looks so much like me. There is just no mistake. The only difference is that while his eyes are as dark as yours, his hair is a little lighter than mine. You'll see!"

Anton took her hand and kissed it. "I only hope that no one else sees the remarkable resemblance to you before we tell him. How am I going to survive until tomorrow afternoon before we see him again!"

"Before we left the reception, I whispered to Jane that we would like to come over tomorrow and talk to Alexei for a few minutes in private, and although she looked surprised, she nodded and said yes."

David opened the apartment door to their knock and let them in with a smile. "Come in, come in," he said with a smile, "Alexei is waiting for you in the parlor. Jane and I are frankly surprised at your particular interest in him, and your request for privacy with him. Anyway, we'll leave you with him and will be in our bedroom until you call us."

"We'll tell you all about it, David, trust me," Anton said in an exuberant tone of voice as they entered the parlor. Alexei rose from where he was sitting and greeted them with a polite nod to Anton and kiss on Lisa's hand. David left the parlor with a soft closing of the bedroom door.

They all remained standing as Anton took Lisa's hand, cleared his throat and said, "Alexei, we came to give you some news that will be shocking. Perhaps we should sit."

Looking at Lisa, then turning his attention to Alexei, he said, "We came to tell you that we are your biological parents. Come, look in this mirror. Do you see how much you look like your mother?"

Alexei gasped. "How can you be sure?" he said as he looked at his and Lisa's images in the mirror.

"My doctor, Dr. Semenov," Lisa said, "delivered you, and now he has done research, concluding that you are, indeed, our son. We were devastated when you were taken from us. I have never gotten over your kidnapping. "

Alexei looked at Lisa, then Anton and slowly nodded, "Yes, I can see a resemblance." Then he turned and with a shy smile put his arms around Lisa, and then Anton, who lost his power of speech and kept gulping tears. When Anton released Alexei from his embrace, his voice shook as he said, "My son... my son, at last we found you! After all these years..."

"From now on I'll be able to bring your images into my memory. My adoptive parents love me, and I love them, so I'll never want to hurt them, but I'm sure they won't object to my seeing you again."

Lisa was the first to come to her senses and said, "We must invite David and Jane to join us and share with them our great news." She knocked on the bedroom door and Jane opened the door. Lisa's radiant face greeted Jane and David as they entered the parlor and invited everyone to sit down, but Anton and Alexei, remained standing.

"Dear friends, I want you to meet our son! After all these years of searching we finally found him in a most unexpected way, here, at Nancy's wedding!"

Jane gasped and rushed over to embrace the young man. Questions poured on Anton, while Lisa watched David. There stood Alesha's biological father, and Dr. Semenov's words knocked painfully in her temple, reminding her that she had deprived her son of his legitimate American citizenship. A wave of guilt overwhelmed her. *This is my Nemesis that I would have to live with forever!*

Jane interrupted Lisa's thoughts with, "David, get the bottle of champagne! We must celebrate this marvelous news over supper together. I can hardly wait to see Serezha's face when we tell him who his brother's biological parents are!"

David came back and filled everyone's glass after inviting them to sit down. Lisa wondered what was on David's mind as he continued to keep the smile that looked artificial now. Was he envious of Anton having a son when he didn't have one? After Jane had Nancy in a breech birth, she was told not to have another pregnancy. Jane had told this to Lisa shortly after Nancy was kidnapped, and they never talked about it. Lisa decided this was the reason for David's seemingly artificial smile.

When supper and busy chatter were over, Lisa and Anton left with promises to have a reunion in Pasadena when Alesha would be visiting there after his graduation.

Lisa couldn't resist hugging her son once more and said, "Alesha, would you come tomorrow to our house for dinner? We can pick you up and bring you back afterward? Our maid, Agasha, used to be your nanny, and you were kidnapped while she took you for a walk. I'm sure she would love to see you now."

"I'd like to, if David and Jane don't mind?"

David was quick to respond, "Of course not. Your old nanny would be happy to see you."

Lisa and Anton smiled broadly, arranged for the hour when they would pick him up the next day, and left the consulate, full of anticipation of spending more time with their son.

On arrival home, Lisa told Agasha about Alexei and that he really was Serezha, and why his name had been changed. The pandemonium that resulted from such news, was loud and happy. Agasha threw her arms up, then made the sign of a cross and cried, "If only I could catch a glimpse of him before he leaves!"

"He's coming for dinner tomorrow, Agasha. We told him about you and he wants to see you too," Anton said with a happy smile.

"Oh, thank you, Barin and Barinya! I'll go and start preparing things for tomorrow!"

～

The next day, when Anton brought Alexei home, Agasha met them at the door, threw herself to her knees, grabbed his hand, and kissed it. Alexei quickly withdrew it and helped her to rise. "I'm so glad to see you too, Agasha. I only wish I could remember things while you took care of me! Was I a good boy?"

"Oh yes, very good, but also very curious!"

Lisa and Anton listened smiling for a while, and then Lisa said, "Agasha that was fun hearing all that, but we're getting a little hungry!"

Agasha got the message immediately and shuffled off to the kitchen. Alexei and his parents exchanged smiles and led Alexei to the parlor. They didn't have to wait long before a tantalizing aroma of borscht was announced and Agasha came in carrying the tureen of the soup.

They savored it, followed by beef stroganoff, accompanied by side dishes of sliced, salted cucumbers swimming in sour cream, and pickled mushrooms glistening in the candelabra's reflection. The dessert was the inevitable homemade ice cream. Alexei described his growing up in a happy environment, spoiled by his adoptive parents who gave him more attention than Serezha. He chuckled here, telling about occasional friction between the brothers. "I had good grades in school, and we were often taken to Imyanpo, where the newlyweds are now," he said at the end of the meal.

"We've never been in Imyanpo," said Anton, "because we vacationed mostly in Handaohedzi."

"Oh. Imyanpo's a beautiful resort," said Alexei, "with a huge park dotted by flower beds and scattered benches, a restaurant overlooking the river, and even croquet and tennis courts for the vacationers. We always had fun there."

"What made you choose mining engineering?" asked Lisa, taking a sip of wine and leaning toward Alexei.

"I've always been interested in learning what is in the depth of our earth and am enjoying my studies."

Time slipped away, and Alexei had to be taken back to Jones' apartment. At the consulate's gate, Lisa hugged Alesha, swallowing tears, knowing that she wouldn't see her son again for quite a long time. Anton coughed slightly and pulled Alexei into his own embrace. "Write to us, dear son, until we see you again."

"I'm sorry to have had so little time with you, but I'm leaving with the happiness to have found you!" Alexei left the car, but not before Lisa handed him a few pictures of herself and Anton, for which he kissed her hand and then stood on the steps of the consulate waving to his parents as the car turned a corner and Lisa and Anton were alone again.

Chapter 17

The visas and all other necessary paperwork were finally in order, and Lisa walked through the half-empty house listlessly, trying not to think of what was waiting for them abroad. Anton tried to prepare her for a much smaller lodging, maybe even just a small apartment, before they'd have time to orient themselves to the area and look for a permanent home.

The inevitable day of departure arrived, and they left their homestead loaded with *piroshki and krendel*, waving to the weeping servants who wished them future happiness in America and sending them several signs of the cross through the air.

At the train station they placed lit candles in the stand in front of St. Nikolas' icon and then boarded the train. As it gathered speed, and the station blurred in the widening distance, Lisa thought irrelevantly, that the candle she lit at the icon would be still flickering while she would no longer see it. She reclined on her seat. No use torturing myself with fears of the future, she thought, and smiled at her husband. Anton reached over and squeezed her hand. His face was drawn and pale, and Lisa felt her heart squeeze with guilt at having ignored him in favor of self-serving pity. But words were intrusive, and both chose to remain silent. Anton kept his sadness hidden within him, for he knew better than upsetting Lisa any more than she was.

When they reached Shanghai, they were overwhelmed by the crowds and the noise, the peddlers selling their wares, the beggars sitting on the sidewalks displaying their festering sores with accompanying singsongs for alms, in spite of the policemen shooing them out of pedestrians' way. The Platonovs were told that their ship would sail the next day, and they were to stay in the elegant Cathay Hotel near the shore of the Whampoo River, where their ship was docked. They liked the hotel, reluctant to venture out where the noise and the heavily populated junks alarmed them in spite of the hotel's entrance being almost a block away. Anton was silent most of the time, for it was obvious he had no comforting words for his wife, being apprehensive himself. Lisa sensed that, and wandered away, leaving him in the lounge where the uniformed high-ranking Japanese officers carried on a serious discussion, while the English and French speaking guests clustered in the opposite side of the room. She tried to concentrate on the oriental decor in various reception halls, and when she came back, she saw that Anton had finished reading the English edition of the Shanghai newspaper, and probably gone to the men's room.

Lisa took that opportunity to sneak outside the front door to look at the display windows. She was immediately surrounded by Chinese urchins dressed in rags with a foul odor, and begging for alms. They tugged at her dress with one of their dirty hands while reaching out with the palm up with the other. Frantic for help, she looked up to see if there was anyone to help extricate her from the attacking children and to her utter surprise saw a Japanese soldier running across the street with revolver pointing at the brazen children. At the sight of the gun, they miraculously scattered away and Lisa looked across the street to thank the soldier, but he was already walking away.

"*Arigato!*" she called out after him, hoping that was the right word for 'thank you.' She backed out of the street and into the safety of the hotel, before Anton returned to the lounge.

A sudden cry of a child from the lobby shook her as she stopped in her tracks and listened. A quiet voice of its mother was soothing the crying baby in Japanese, and a different wave of thoughts overwhelmed Lisa. She hurried into the lobby, but the child had stopped crying. The agony of fearing the incestuous marriage to take place had evaporated, and she should have been elated and grateful to fate for lifting that huge burden off her shoulders. Her son was studying in Australia to get a profitable degree. How proud she was of him! She would see him again, now that she would be living in America, and away from hunghuzi and the Japanese occupation. *Time to dwell on positive thoughts*. With a firm step, Lisa headed back into the lounge looking for Anton to try to make him feel in a better mood.

He came back into the lounge and noticed her change of attitude. Before she was able to say a word, he smiled and said, "Well, what caused such a sudden change in my *golubka?*"

Lisa swallowed hard and thought how stupid of her to show her glee in her face. She couldn't tell him why, and had to continue hiding the truth about Serezha's birth forever.

"Just changed my trend of thoughts, darling, to the good things awaiting us, especially our reunion with all the Joneses in Southern California.

"I'm sure happy to see you smiling, *golubka.*"

In the reflecting light of the end table lamp, Anton's face looked pale and drawn, and Lisa felt overwhelmed by guilt for not having paid more attention to her husband. She spent the rest of the slow-moving day entertaining him with memories of the past happy holidays and then remembered the hours spent playing chess with him when she nearly won, but always lost in the end.

Anton actually laughed in reminiscing about those days and as the day ended with a delicious meal of steak with mushrooms and salad, they retired for the night, to be ready to leave China in the morning. A twinge of sadness scratched Anton's chest nonetheless, as that clear fact kept him from falling asleep for a long time... they would be leaving behind everything he loved in Manchuria, and probably would never see it again. Unclear dreams followed until an alarm clock woke them both with a start. Lisa confessed to the same ghostly dreams, but there was no time to discuss them and they concentrated on getting ready to have a hurried breakfast and leave the hotel to board the ship.

After they checked in onboard the ship, they came out and leaned over the railing, clasping each other's hands. In silence they watched as the ship moved away from the dock and detached itself from the last contact with China, causing the muddy Whampoo to wobble in tiny waves. They watched the ship slice through the tightly squeezed junks full of Chinese families waving at them, until several junks started to fall back one by one until the last one turned away from the ship and hugged the shore to disappear behind them.

They stayed on deck until the river brought them to the open sea to start their journey to the New World.